Nerd No More

Nerd No More

Kristine L. Franklin

A TRUMPET CLUB SPECIAL EDITION

ISBN 0-590-21804-2

Copyright © 1996 by Kristine L. Franklin. All rights reserved.
Published by Scholastic Inc., 555 Broadway, New York, NY 10012,
by arrangement with Candlewick Press. TRUMPET and associated logos are
trademarks and/or registered trademarks of Scholastic Inc.

12 11 10 9 8 7 6 5 4 3 2   4 5 6 7 8 9/0

Printed in the U.S.A.   40

First Scholastic printing, January 1998

This book was typeset in Slimbach.

To Kelly,
with much love
from Mom
/ \ /
Thanks for putting up with
all the weird foreign food.

Chapter One

I never asked to be a nerd. It just happened. I used to be a regular kid, Wiggie V. Carter, the guy who could flick bottle caps from the door of Mr. Bell's sixth-grade classroom all the way to the girls' can. I was smart, straight As actually, but it was no big deal. People hardly noticed.

Then Mom took the job at Channel 62 and everything changed. Suddenly I was famous. Way too famous. The wrong kind of famous. And it was all Mom's fault.

To me, Marilyn M. Carter, B.S., M.S., Ph.D., is just Mom. She's super smart, and she's not bad looking when she takes off her glasses. She likes classical music and weird foreign food, but who's perfect? On a scale from one to ten, I'd give her a nine, but only because of all the tofu enchiladas and moo goo gai pan she tries to make me eat. Everyone calls my mom Dr. Carter, everyone but the kids at school. They call her Mrs. Science. And I'm her son.

Every Wednesday and Friday morning at ten on goes the TV, right after Mr. Bell makes us sing "My Country 'Tis of Thee" so we'll grow up to be patriotic Americans. Twice a week we have to watch this educational science show, which wouldn't be too bad except for the fact that the educational TV science show scientist happens to be *my* mom in living color, lab coat, glasses, microscope, the works.

"Good morning, girls and boys," she always says in a fakey excited voice. "It's time to JUMP into science!" That's when I wish I were small enough to hide in a jar of paste.

It wasn't too bad until she got to single-celled animals. Then, right on TV, in front of a million other sixth graders, my mom showed microscope pictures of amoebas and told how they can infest your *bowels*.

Why did she have to use that word? Why couldn't she say intestines or stomach or guts? The same day, this new kid, Eddie Grzinovich, started calling me Bowel Boy. It wouldn't have been so bad if Billy Lopez hadn't laughed his head off and started calling me Bowel Boy, too. Billy and I used to be best friends. Once, in third grade, I traded him a live frog from my mom's lab for a 1972 Corvette Stingray Matchbox Car. It was neon pink. When the frog died, I gave him back the car. Last year Billy taught me all the words to "La Bamba" in Spanish. I showed him how to make a cannon out of two tennis ball cans taped together. Last year and the year before, Billy and I were locker partners. We played basketball just about every day after school in our alley. This year for the first week of school, we were locker partners again, but then Eddie Grzinovich moved next door to Billy and those two started hanging out all the time and Billy told me he was going to be locker partners with Eddie instead. Big deal. I got the locker to myself. No more smelling Billy's dirty P.E. socks, right?

After that, Billy started dressing like Eddie. He bought the same Maxi-Jump basketball shoes and started wearing a Seahawks football jacket with real leather sleeves. He even got his ear pierced. I guess laughing and calling me Bowel Boy was part of Billy's new coolness. How could he be such a traitor? By lunchtime the whole school was calling me Bowel Boy. But Bowel Boy was just the beginning.

Kids started humming the *Jump Into Science* music whenever I walked by. Eddie Grzinovich asked when was I going to wear my lab coat to school. Jennifer Davis drew a picture of a skinny brown-haired kid with big glasses and a laptop computer and a pocket protector full of BIC four-color pens and taped it to my desk. CLASS NERD it said at the top. No mistaking who that calculator kid was supposed to be. Me. Wiggie V. Son of Mrs. Science.

I thought if I got rid of my glasses they'd leave me alone. Glasses do give a guy a sort of studious appearance. I begged my mom to buy me contacts, but she said eleven is too young. I tried another strategy. I started forgetting my homework. I made stupid mistakes in my math worksheets. I turned in papers without my name written at the top. I wanted to show I was like all the rest of them. Once when Mr.

Bell called on me during science, I answered wrong on purpose. "Wiggie," said Mr. Bell. "What kind of skeleton does an insect have?"

"Crunchy," I answered, and everyone laughed. I knew it was exoskeleton, but I had a point to prove. Mr. Bell *knew* I knew the right answer. How could I not? I mean, my mom is Mrs. Science! That makes me Jr. Science, right? Mr. Bell gave me a laziness lecture and called Mom about all my sloppy schoolwork. That got me no TV for a week. If we had Nintendo, she would have taken that away too, but we're the only kids in the world without it. Mom says she doesn't want us to turn into vidiots. Some days I would give anything to be a vidiot.

I tried talking to the other kids about video games anyway, like I knew all about them. Next to basketball, video games are the hottest topic among sixth-grade boys. I told them my favorites were DynoDonkey Destruction and BugGutz. I bragged that I knew all the moves, all the tricks. I wore a Band-Aid on my thumb and said I had a firing-button blister. It didn't make any difference. They kept calling me names. Bowel Boy. Nerd. Mad Scientist. I was marked. To the rest of the world I was nothing but a jerk. No amount of faking helped.

Then Callie came.

"Class," said Mr. Bell, "I'd like you all to meet Callie Adams."

It was a Monday, the first of October, and we were gluing glitter on stupid paper masks. Second-grade stuff, if you ask me. My little brother would have loved it. He would have swiped some of the glitter so he could check it out under his microscope. The new girl, Callie, took the empty desk next to mine. I checked her out. She was real small, wearing a too-big red sweatshirt with an orange-and-purple striped skirt. Colorblind, I guessed. Her skirt hung crooked from her skinny waist and her rear end was dirty, like she'd slid down a mud bank or something. Her socks had fallen down around her ankles and her shoelaces sprawled around her feet untied. She was a mess!

"My name's Wiggie Carter," I said. I didn't tell her my full, actual name. It's not like it's a secret or anything, just not one of the things I like to broadcast, especially not when other people are in a name-calling mood. "Did you just move here?"

"No," said Callie. She shoved her notebooks, papers, crayons, pencils, and a long blue ruler into her desk. Then she laid out the sheets of construction paper for our art project and started cutting. Right away I could tell she was making a pumpkin shape. I made three piles of spilled glitter and peeked at Callie out of the corner of my eye. Her hair was braided in messy rows down the sides of her head. I wondered if she'd done them herself. I counted them. Seven little rows on each side and one down the back. Something about those rows looked familiar.

"Did you get kicked out of Mrs. Anderson's class?" I asked. Mrs. Anderson is the other sixth-grade teacher.

"Hardly," said Callie. "Pass the orange, please." I passed her the orange glitter and put a squiggle of Elmer's on my Mutilated Mummy Mask. So far it was mostly green, for decay. I poured red glitter on the glue for blood and smooshed it down with my finger.

"Mummies didn't bleed, you know," said Callie without looking up. She filled in the pumpkin's stem with a huge blop of glue and rubbed it around with her finger. "Mummies were *desiccated*. Filled with preservative spices and resins and dried out." Callie wiped her gluey finger on her skirt. "May I please have the green glitter?" I passed her the green glitter, my mouth hanging open like a dumb cartoon guy. *Desiccated?* Then I remembered where I'd seen Callie before.

"You're a *fifth* grader!" I practically shouted. "I've seen you at Mrs. Chin's lunch table."

"Wrong again," said Callie. She sprinkled the pumpkin stem with green glitter. Some of it fell on the desk. Some of it fell on the floor. Lots of it fell in Callie's lap. Then she cut out triangle eyes and a snaggletoothed mouth. "I'm a sixth grader as of today. I've been advanced."

"What are you, some kind of genius?" I asked. I quickly wiped the glue and red glitter from the Mutilated Desiccated Preserved-with-Spices-and-Resins Mummy Mask.

"Maybe," said Callie. She blew on the wet glue and glitter to dry them.

"Too bad," I said. Being Son of Mrs. Science was

definitely uncomfortable, but being a genius had to be worse. Everyone hates a genius.

"I know you," said Callie without looking up. "You're Bowel Boy." Suddenly being a mere genius didn't seem so unattractive.

"They only call me that because my mom does *Jump Into Science* on Channel 62," I said. "She did a lesson on parasites. You know, amoebas?"

"That's your mom?" Callie stopped cutting and stared at me. Somehow, she'd gotten a bunch of green glitter on her chin. "Wow! Really?"

"Yeah, really." I wiped some extra glue on my pants.

"That's a great show," said Callie. She started cutting again. "You are super lucky to have such a famous mom."

"Yeah, real lucky," I said. "Everyone says I'm a nerd because my mom is a scientist."

"What's wrong with that?" asked Callie.

"What's wrong with being a nerd? Are you serious?" Was this girl clueless or what? NO one wants to be a nerd.

"No, I mean being a scientist. What's wrong with that? I think it's exciting."

"Maybe for my mom it's exciting." Mom doesn't mind being a nerd. I don't even think she *knows* she's a nerd. Maybe that's because all her friends are nerds too. They *have* to be. They're all scientists.

"Your mom must be super smart."

"Yeah, I guess," I said. So am I, but I didn't tell Callie. Was it my fault I learned to read when I was two? Was it my fault Mom taught me fractions in kindergarten, when I was too little to know the difference between a fun game and *math*? It wasn't the kind of thing I wanted spread around.

"I bet you're smart too," said Callie. I shrugged. "Did you skip a grade too? Is that why the kids make fun of you?"

I picked at a piece of glitter under my thumbnail. "They wanted me to skip second grade," I said, practically whispering. I looked around to see if anyone was listening. "Mom wouldn't let me. Too much happened that year, uh, family stuff, a sort of tragedy." Callie nodded. I concentrated on my mask. I could feel her looking at me. I felt my ears turn red. My throat got tight. My heart thumped at my temples. Why'd I tell her all that?

"Maybe the other kids tease you because they have a wrong image of you," said Callie.

"What do you mean?" I asked.

"Maybe you should try to help people see that you aren't who they think you are." Callie poked two holes in the sides of her pumpkin mask. "If everyone thinks you're a nerd, and you aren't, maybe it's because people don't see you for who you are. Maybe you could work on your image. You know, get a new one."

"A new *image*?" Before, when I was a regular kid who got straight As, I never thought about who I was. I never thought about my image, about what other people thought of me. I watched Callie tie a long piece of string to each hole on her mask. She held up the jack-o'-lantern mask to her face. Her dark eyes sparkled at me through the eyeholes.

"If you don't like your image," said Callie's lips through the snaggletoothed hole, "do something about it."

I definitely hated my current image. It would be nice to be someone else.

No more Bowel Boy? No more Son of Mrs.

Science? No more nerd? Was it possible to change what people thought of me? Was it really as simple as putting on a Halloween mask?

I grabbed my Mutilated Mummy Mask and held it up to my face and looked out. "Hey, maybe you *are* a genius!" I said behind the paper and crayon lips.

"Takes one to know one," said Callie. She put down her mask and grinned at me. A speck of orange glitter sparkled on her front tooth.

Chapter Two

I ran home after school, down Forty-sixth Street, past the big chestnut tree and across Mr. Bataglia's front yard. I had to keep pushing up my glasses with one finger to keep them from slipping off, but it didn't slow me down. The regular shortcut through the alley was blocked by Mr. Jazinik's RV, so I scrambled over Nicky Thompson's fence, cut across the corner of his backyard, jumped over the roses, and landed in my own backyard. I checked my shoes. Clean landing.

"Hey, Foof," I yelled. "I'm gonna get a new image!" Foofie was lying like a dead dog on the top of the 55-gallon drum my mom uses for growing mosquito larvae. He gets up there by going from the low brick wall around the flower garden to the picnic bench to the picnic table to the drum. Foofie thumped his tail once and went back to sleep. By the look on his face, he was in the middle of a good dream. Probably rolling in a dead skunk.

The screen door was hanging open. I hopped over a red plastic stethoscope and banged on the back door. "It's me!" I yelled. "Open up." I heard quick footsteps and then my little brother, Wolfie, opened the door.

"Don't make so much noise," lisped Wolfie through the gap in his front teeth. "Mom's working in the lab downstairs." I brushed past him and dropped my books on the kitchen counter.

"Mom's always working," I said. "That's all she does." I opened the fridge and drained the nearest milk carton. "She never watches TV, never goes to movies, never goes to the mall, never hardly even laughs. I'll never be a scientist." I opened a new carton of milk and took a swig.

Wolfie looked up at me through his little wire-rimmed glasses. "Dad was a scientist."

"Yeah," I said. "And look how *he* ended up. Dead on a glacier with a pocket full of slime." Wolfie's eyes bulged. He put his hands on his hips and stuck his chin out at me.

"Don't you talk about Dad that way!" he sputtered.

"Sorry, sorry, Wolf," I said. I put my hands together like I was praying and bowed down to him. "I beg you to forgive me." Then I messed up his hair. Wolfie's still stuck in hero-worship mode about Dad. Maybe it's because he hardly knew him.

When my dad died it was on TV and everything. I still have a newspaper clipping. I remember it pretty well, even though I was only a second grader. See, Dad was in Alaska, heading up a research team that was studying some kind of algae that grows only in the snowpack on Mount Denali. One of the other team members fell down a crevasse. Dad went down after him. Dad saved the other guy, but the others weren't able to save *him*. According to everyone, that makes him a hero. When Mom told me the news I didn't care if he was a hero or not. I just wanted him to come back.

"Wolfie," I said, trying to explain, "I don't want to spend my whole life squinting at green scum balls under a microscope. From now on I want a totally new image." I grabbed an open package of Oreos and put a three-stack in my mouth. Wolfie stared at me with his mouth open. I plugged the hole with a two-stack.

"I still want to be a scientist," said Wolfie, puffing cookie crumbs out with every word. "Like Dad and Mom."

"Great, Wolf," I said through my own crumbs. "I'm happy for you."

My brother, Wolfie, is the only kid in the second grade with his own chemistry set. First it was invisible ink. Then it was shampoo cupcakes, which he baked with the hair dryer. Once he painted the kitchen floor with a liquid explosive that popped and smoked when we walked on it. Mom grounded him for a week, but I could tell she was proud. Wolfie is a science kid, one hundred percent.

Not me. No way. From now on I was going to be the opposite of a science kid, no matter what it took.

I was getting a new image. No more lab coat and cal-culator jokes for me.

I finished my Oreos, grabbed a couple for later, punched Wolfie a light one on the shoulder, and went up to my room. I had a ton of work to do.

Later, when I smelled something garlicky and dis-gusting I knew dinner was almost ready. My mom, who cooks up all kinds of perfect chemical formu-las, has never figured out how to fix a decent meal. Right after Dad died, we ate out almost every night. Now *that* was food. Big Macs, deep dish pizza, KFC Extra Crispy, lots and lots of french fries. Then Mom decided she needed a new hobby. She bought a book called *Cooking Around the World* and pretty soon this so-called *food* started showing up on our plates and we quit eating out. I tried to tell her that if I'd wanted to eat deep-fried millet balls and peanut soup, I would have been born in Ghana, but she didn't lis-ten. It's a wonder I've grown an inch since then.

I waited for Mom to call me for dinner. I was in no hurry to eat her latest pile of organic debris. I had other things to do. I was busy getting my new image together. I heard a tap on my bedroom door.

"Wig?" said Wolfie, outside my door. "Dinner."

"What country?" I asked.

"Italy," came the reply. "Mom said to tell you it's *risi e bisi*." I sighed. What about canned ravioli, or even spaghetti? Now *that's* Italian. Good thing I was still stuffed from Oreos and milk.

"Okay, okay," I said. "I'll be right down." I had a couple more things to take care of before dinner. Everything had to be ready for school in the morning. I couldn't leave a single detail until the last minute.

"What are you doing, Wiggie?" asked Wolfie through the door. I heard the doorknob turn.

"Don't come in!" I shouted, but it was too late. Wolfie peeked around the door and when he saw me, his mouth dropped open.

"Sunglasses?" he finally said, but I was already pushing him out the door.

"It's bright in here, okay?" I said, slamming the door behind him and shoving my fake lizard skin beanbag chair in front of the door. I piled a bunch of encyclopedias on top of it for weight. "Just keep your mouth shut or I'll tell Mom what happened to all the Jell-O and rubbing alcohol."

"I was trying to make a new kind of plastic!" wailed Wolfie from the other side of my door.

"I'm not kidding," I said, stripping off my clothes. "You'd better not tell."

"I won't tell," said the little voice beyond the door. I messed up my hair to look normal, tossed a towel over the stuff on the bed, threw on a pair of sweats, and shoved the beanbag chair full of encyclopedias out of my way. Wolfie was waiting outside the door. "I won't tell," he said. And then he whispered, "Was that your new image?"

My face stretched tight in an out-of-control grin. "Yeah," I said, and hurried downstairs two steps at a time. Foofie was sprawled across the bottom step. I jumped over him and hit the floor with a thump.

Just wait until they saw me. The *new,* formal, cultured, grown-up, aloof, and completely reorganized me. I'd make an entrance they'd never forget.

Good-bye, Jr. Science. Hello, new image. Tomorrow they'd see the new Wiggie V. Carter.

No. Wait. I lifted up my sunglasses and looked at my reflection in the mirror.

From now on I'd be using my real name. No more hiding the real me. It was my heritage, my destiny. Tomorrow the world would meet the one and only original Ludwig van Beethoven Carter.

Chapter Three

"Uh-oh," said Callie the next morning. "Looks like somebody died." She looked me up and down as we walked into class. "Are you going to a funeral, or what?" she asked. It was ten minutes before class and Billy and Eddie were out playing basketball. Good thing they didn't ask me to play. I was hardly dressed for basketball. I slid into my chair and smoothed down my black tuxedo jacket. Mom had the tux made for me when I was in my aunt Ginny's wedding last June. It's the kind with tails, like Bugs Bunny wears when he leads an orchestra. It still fit fine. I straightened the cummerbund. I ran a comb through my slicked-down hair.

"No funeral," I said. "I'm just being myself." I spoke in my best English accent. "After all, I *am* Ludwig van Beethoven Carter." A couple of girls came into the room. I saw them notice me.

Callie scrunched up her nose. *"Ludwig?"*

"It's a long-standing tradition in my mother's family," I explained. "Everyone on my mother's side of the family has a famous name. For instance, my mother's maiden name was Monroe. Get it? Marilyn Monroe. Grandpa was James Monroe."

Callie looked puzzled. "But *Ludwig*? Nobody names their kid Ludwig."

I cleared my throat to explain. "My parents met at the symphony, so when I was born they decided to name their children after famous musicians. My brother's name is Wolfgang."

"As in Mozart?" asked Callie.

"Precisely." For the first time in my life I felt distinguished, high class. The name Ludwig was much better for my image than Wiggie. It was cultured. Sophisticated. A billion miles away from test tubes and hydrochloric acid. For the first time in my life I had a reason to be proud of my name.

Just then Eddie came through the door. Billy was right behind him. They were both sweaty. They probably smelled pretty bad.

A pencil rolled off Callie's desk and hit the floor with a snap. She reached over and picked it up. She dug a pink pencil sharpener out of her desk and started sharpening the pencil.

I carefully loosened each finger of my white gloves, removed them with dignity and a ton of culture. I laid them carefully inside my desk. I straightened my tie.

"My grandma has white gloves," said Callie. "She wears them to church on Easter." I suddenly felt hot. I was glad my dark glasses covered at least part of my face.

"They're conductor's gloves," I said loudly, straightening my tie again and hoping that conductors wear gloves. "You see, Callie," I said, "classical music is my life." Actually, I don't know that much about classical music. Mom's the one who loves listening to cello trios and fat screaming opera divas and choirs that sing only in foreign languages. OK, I did know a little something about it. Mom bought us *Fantasia* the minute it came out in video.

The classroom was almost full. I looked high class and people were starting to notice. Kids were whispering all around. I was making an incredible impression. Callie shrugged and rolled her eyes. "Your image should be natural," she said. "A kid image."

"I can't possibly imagine what you mean," I said. "I look perfectly natural."

"Yeah," said Callie, "about as natural as Dracula."

Just then Mr. Bell walked in. Everyone got quiet, as if Mrs. Jefferson, the principal, had walked into the class instead of Mr. Bell. Mr. Bell saw me, stared, and blinked twice. Allison Koppelman snorted.

"Sun too bright today, Wiggie?" asked Mr. Bell. The whole class laughed. It was one of those drizzle days. Outside it was so dark you'd hardly know it was day. Mr. Bell is the best teacher I've ever had. I hoped he'd like my new image.

"It's these fluorescent lights, sir," I said. When I said "sir" I sounded just like the butler in an English murder mystery. I was good. I knew man teachers love to be called "sir." "And if you don't mind, sir," I said, "please call me Ludwig from now on. It is my real name, you know."

Mr. Bell's eyebrows shot up. He polished his bald head with one hand and looked stern, but I could tell he was trying not to smile. He bit his lower lip. The right side of his face twitched. "All right, Ludwig," said Mr. Bell and then we started right in on math. It wasn't until recess that the trouble began.

"Hey, EAR-wig," said Eddie Grzinovich. "Nice tie." The other kids were playing foursquare in the school basement. On rainy days we have to play inside, but because of my new image, I wasn't interested in foursquare. I didn't want to mess up my tux. I also couldn't see very well with sunglasses. Right away the other kids started chanting "EAR-wig, EAR-wig," and then Eddie ran by and pulled on my bow tie.

He didn't pull hard. It was just a tug. But it was enough of a tug to unsnap the clip and jerk my tie from my collar. I tried to grab it but Billy snatched it from the floor and ran.

All of a sudden about a hundred kids were playing keep-away with my tie. Billy put it under his nose like a mustache. Allison and a redheaded girl from Mrs. Anderson's class grabbed my tie from Billy and played catch. Eddie jumped up like he was going to do a slam-dunk, snatched my tie from between the girls, and ran. "Boys rule!" he yelled. There was nothing left to do. My dignity disappeared.

"Give me back my tie, you garbage-faced geeks!" I yelled.

"EAR-wig, EAR-wig," chanted the kids. Eddie Grzinovich had my tie tucked under his foul armpit.

"Hey, NERDWIG," shouted Eddie. "Come and get your clip-on tie. Baby necktie! Baby necktie! Wanna pacifier?" He tossed my tie above his head. "Yee-haw!"

I dove for his legs.

The next thing I remember was Eddie's eighty-dollar Maxi-Jump high-top leather basketball shoe smashing into my nose. After that there was a lot of blood and yelling and then angry grown-up voices. Eddie and I ended up in Mrs. Jefferson's office.

I held an ice pack to my nose. Eddie held one to the back of his head.

"Okay, boys," said Mrs. Jefferson. "Who started it?" I think her eyes were brown. I think they were boring into me. It was hard to be sure. Somewhere along the way I'd lost my prescription sunglasses. I'd begged Mom for those glasses. She was going to kill me.

What I could see was a blurry gray-haired lady with bowling balls for boobs, leaning toward us on a desk with a lot of papers and an olive-green telephone. The effect was terrifying. On top of that, Mrs. Jefferson is known around school as the General. If she has any niceness at all, it never shows. I didn't say a word. Neither did Eddie.

We didn't get suspended but we did get detention. A week's worth of blackboards after school. We had to start that day. Mrs. Jefferson told us that if we got caught fighting again we'd be suspended for three days. We'd also get a visit from the cops from the juvenile crime division. She said words like "assault" and "battery" and "willful harm." I've never been in trouble before. I forced my lower lip not to quiver. I forced myself not to look at Eddie. Eddie who stole my best friend.

Worst of all, right before she said we could go, the General told us Mr. Bell was going to call our moms to explain why we would be late from school for the next week. He'd tell Mom about the tie. Then he'd tell her about my tux and the dark glasses and maybe even the accent. And Ludwig. Then I'd have to explain about my new image.

And why I hated the old one so much.

Chapter Four

I erased blackboards until four o'clock and started for home. The rain dripped off my throbbing nose. It soaked my jacket. It made spots and streaks in the chalk dust on my sleeves.

Someone had found my tie. I stuffed it in my pocket along with the gloves. My prescription sunglasses never showed up. A gust of wind blew in my face and I shivered. Wet fallen leaves dotted the sidewalk, but I could hardly see them. I didn't hurry. Wolfie had been home since three. Mr. Bell had had plenty of time to call. Mom would be waiting.

I got in the back door without being noticed. So

far, so good. The rain was really beating down now, pattering against the roof and running down the windows in rivers. I slid Foofie out of the way of the refrigerator door with my foot. He didn't wake up.

I took out the milk and just as I was about to take a big refreshing straight-from-the-carton swig, I heard Mom's footsteps on the basement stairs. I swung open the cupboard and grabbed a glass. Close call.

"Wiggie?" said Mom. "Is that you? How come you're so late?" She opened the door and took one look. Her mouth dropped open and I thought for sure her glasses would slide right off her nose. "What happened?"

I hadn't come ready to explain. I'd figured Wolfie would have told her the whole story by now. And hadn't Mr. Bell called yet?

"I got in some trouble at school," I said. "Didn't Wolfie tell you?" Mom was looking hard. She squinted.

"Wolfie's at Cub Scouts."

How could I have forgotten? Then I remembered

something else. Mr. Bell coaches Pee Wee football after school. There was still time.

"Why are you dressed like that?" asked Mom. "And where are your glasses?" Her own glasses make her eyes look big. They got even bigger.

I didn't want to explain. Not yet. My nose hurt. My hair was wet. My glass of milk was making my hand cold. I tried to make my eyes look pitiful. It's a trick I learned from Foofie. It's a lot easier to do when you aren't wearing glasses. Mom's face softened immediately.

"What happened to your nose?" Mom came close, about six inches away from my face. She took hold of my chin and turned my head from side to side. Her hands smelled like rubber gloves. "Did someone *hit* you?"

Mom's voice had that high, quavery, concerned sound. I let out a big sigh. I was out of the woods, at least for now. No decent mom would yell at a kid with a golf ball for a nose and pitiful basset hound eyes.

"Yeah," I said, sniffing. "Eddie Grzinovich kicked

me." When I said "me" it came out like "be." I drank the milk. I watched Mom over the rim of the glass. She was shaking her head and frowning at that lowlife scum Eddie. I could tell.

"Eddie who? Good grief, Wiggie," said Mom, "that's horrible. Can you tell me what happened?" Her voice was gentle. Her eyes were sad, but not as sad as mine. I shook my head. That bought me some time. It also made my nose start throbbing again. Tears came to my eyes.

"That's okay, honey," said Mom quickly. She put one arm around me and steered me to the stairs. "Go upstairs and get cleaned up. I'll bring you some aspirin and when you feel better, we'll talk."

Time. There was still time. I walked up the stairs, careful not to jiggle my aching head and nose. When I got to my room I quickly stripped off my wet clothes and threw them in the closet. Maybe she would feel so sorry about my nose that she'd forget about the tux.

I put on my Seahawks sweatpants and sweatshirt and climbed into bed. I thought about what to tell my mom. When I heard her coming up the stairs I groaned. It was an honest groan.

Mom sat on my bed and handed me the aspirin and a glass of water. I gagged down the aspirin and wiped my mouth on my sleeve. Mom looked at me through her glasses with that I'm-waiting-to-hear-it-all look. I took a deep breath and told her everything, mostly.

"I wore my tux to school, you know, the one from the wedding, because I thought it would be fun to dress up for once, see, and Eddie, he stole my tie, and pretty soon other kids were running around with it and I had to save it, didn't I? I mean, it *is* my only bow tie. I think they were jealous because I was dressed up and they looked like such a bunch of grunges, because before I knew it I was lying on the floor with Eddie's shoe up my nose, and then we were sent to the office and Mrs. Jefferson stared at us until we couldn't say anything, but now we have to do blackboards. For a week. For fighting."

"You got kicked in the face for wearing a tux to school?" Mom was still frowning at my story. She didn't get it.

"Yeah," I said. "And my tie. And gloves."

"Gloves?" I nodded. Mom took a deep breath.

"Okay, let me get this straight. You wore your tux to school, and someone kicked you in the face because another kid took your necktie?" She was still frowning.

"Yeah." I twiddled with my covers. Mom sighed and turned away.

"Why on earth did you wear a tux to school?"

That's the question I couldn't answer. I couldn't tell her about not wanting to be a nerd. I couldn't tell her that she was the reason everyone was cutting on me. I couldn't tell her how much I needed a new image.

I kept twiddling the sheets. I didn't say anything. Mom just sat there. She put her face in her hands and shook her head slowly, from side to side, for about a year and a half. Then she said it. She said it quietly, but I heard her. I can't believe she said it.

"I wish your dad were here."

All of a sudden my eyes were watering like crazy, running down the sides of my head and into my ears. My throat swelled up and I couldn't breathe, not unless I started blubbering, and I couldn't blubber, not with Mom there.

I have to be tough so Mom won't cry. About Dad, that is. It's been that way for a long time. And I'm pretty tough. I've had a lot of practice not blubbering. But with a throbbing nose and being a nerd and not having a decent image and on top of it missing my dad like crazy—

I swallowed hard. I bit my lip. I felt the blubbers coming.

The phone rang.

Mom got up and went to her room. I heard her pick up the phone. I did a bunch of fast breathing, to get rid of the choking feeling in my neck.

"This is Dr. Carter," said Mom. A pause. "Oh, hi, Mr. Bell," she said, and then there was a lot of "uh-huh" and "I see" and then "that's a shame," and then she said, "Of course I'm still on for Friday. I'm looking forward to it." I listened so hard my ears hurt. "Friday morning, eight sharp," said Mom into the phone in her room. "Oh, me too," she said, and then, "good-bye," and the phone went click into its cradle. I waited for her to come bawl me out.

"Who was that, Mom?" I called, like I didn't

already know. Mom stopped at my door and stuck her head in.

"It was Mr. Bell," said Mom. "He said he was sorry about your getting kicked by Eddie. He said this Eddie kid is a real rough one; it was probably his fault." I cheered for Mr. Bell in my heart.

"He also wanted to remind me about the field trip this Friday." My cheering heart started booing and hissing. How could I have forgotten? As if TV Mom wasn't enough.

Mom was going on a field trip with our class.

Mr. Bell had asked her clear back when school started. Now everyone would see her in the flesh, specimen jars and all, thanks to Mr. Bell and his big ideas. "Mr. Bell invited me to ride on the bus with the class up to Mount Rainier National Park. Wasn't that nice?"

"A lot of people puke when they ride the bus, Mom. You should drive." It was a lame attempt to dissuade her, but then, my mom isn't scared of puke. Absolutely nothing grosses her out, except rude manners.

"Wiggie," said Mom with a frown. "The word is

vomit." She straightened my covers and told me to rest until dinner. She closed the door softly as she left.

I was in a panic. I had to think fast. My face was hurting. My stomach too. Thinking about Mom riding the bus made my stomach hurt. Rest was the last thing on my mind. I had thinking and planning to do. I had to get a new image, *now.*

As soon as the other kids saw all my mom's jars and tweezers and magnifying glasses and permanent ink markers for writing on plastic bags, I'd be a nerd-by-association for the rest of my life. Other teachers took their students on field trips to the bakery or the post office or the police station. Not ours. Not Mr. Bell. He had to have an all-out, real scientific expedition, complete with a real scientist. When the kids found out about her specialty, I mean her *real* specialty, the thing she likes to study more than anything else, the thing she earned her Ph.D. studying . . . just thinking about it caused waves of panic to rise up from my bellybutton.

See, my mom isn't just any old wildlife biologist. Nope, it's worse than that. Big word, bad news. *Parasitology.* The study of parasites, the internal and external kinds that birds and mammals get. We're talking fleas and lice, bowels, bladders, blood, and a lot of poop and pee. Beakers and petri dishes full of it. Smears on glass slides and test tubes in the centrifuge. Smells you wouldn't believe. They would never understand. Never, ever, ever.

My heart was racing. I was desperate. The new me had to be stunning, unforgettable. It had to wipe the nerd image out the minds of everyone before Friday. I had to get Eddie Grzinovich off my case and I had to do it now.

I ignored my gigantic pounding nose, crawled out of bed, and started digging in my closet.

Chapter Five

I spent half the night thinking of a better image.
Finally, around midnight, it came to me in a flash.
Then I could hardly sleep because I was so excited.
Why hadn't I thought of it sooner? Mom left before
I got up the next day. She leaves early on Wednesdays
so she can get to the University of Washington in time
to teach her classes. It's a good thing. If she'd seen
me, she would never have let me out the door. Wolfie
said he was going to tell, until I promised to scoop the
yard after Foofie for a whole month. It was worth it.
My improved image would knock them flat. Being a
classical music snob was way too close to being a

nerd. This new, better image was a million miles from scientific. I couldn't wait to get to school.

Sure, a few kids stared, but no one said anything as I slid into my chair. Mr. Bell was reading something, so he didn't notice. Some of the kids were giggling. Callie stared with her mouth open. I smiled and winked at her, posing and looking as natural as possible. She was wearing denim overalls. One of the straps was undone and hung over the back of her chair.

"What do you think?" I finally asked her.

"How much glue did it take to get your hair to do that?" she asked.

I reached up and felt my perfectly pointed spike. It was sharp. So was I. "I used Spike Stuff," I said. "Half a jar."

"Nice glitter," said Callie. "It adds a definite sparkle to your personality."

I grinned. I'd scraped the rest of the glitter off my Mutilated Mummy Mask and sprinkled it on the Spike Stuff when it was still wet. "What am I supposed to call you today?" Callie asked.

"Lud," I said. "It rhymes with blood." Callie scrunched up her nose.

"That's gross."

"I'm thinking of starting a rock band." I said. "I'm still working on the name."

"Can you play the guitar?" asked Callie.

"Nah."

"Drums?"

"Nah."

"So what are you going to play?"

"Vocals," I said. "I'm quite talented vocally."

"So, you're this great singer?" asked Callie.

"In a rock band singing and vocals aren't the same," I explained. "Totally different talents, actually." I picked up my pencil and pretended it was a microphone. "Yelling is what counts," I said. "And shaking your head all around." I shook my head. My hair didn't move.

"Where did you get the necklace?" asked Callie.

"I got it from my dog, Foofie." I fingered the metal-studded leather collar around my neck. "It kind of stinks but I'm used to it now."

Just then Mr. Bell looked up and saw me for the first time and for a second he had that trying-not-to-crack-up bulging mouth look. He took roll and when he got to me I told him to call me Lud. He nodded but didn't say anything about my new image. We said the Pledge of Allegiance and read about the tundra and then it was time for *Jump Into Science*.

"Hey," said Eddie, "It's Bowel Boy's mommy!" Mr. Bell yelled at Eddie. I slumped way down in my chair and didn't look once at Mom.

Finally the torture was over. Mr. Bell reminded us about the field trip and asked if anyone had brought back a signed permission slip. "Now we get to see Mrs. Bowels in person," said Eddie, and everyone stared at me and laughed until Mr. Bell made them shut up. Callie's overalls' strap caught on her desk when she got up to hand in her permission slip and a couple of girls snickered. For once they weren't laughing at me. I was glad for the distraction because at that moment my face was as flaming as a torch. *Mrs. Bowels*. That creep. I dug my unsigned, crumpled-up permission slip out of my desk and stuffed it in my pocket. Then I ran out the door for P.E.

I changed into my sweatpants and was retying my shoes when Eddie said, "Hey, Fido! Woof woof," and touched my spiked hair. He acted like he cut himself. "Very sharp hair, man," he said. Then he did an air guitar in his underwear and all the guys cracked up. Pretty soon everyone was doing an air guitar, even Billy. I grinned. Hey! They liked my new image! Lud was a hit!

We ran out to the field. I was feeling pretty pumped up. If we had teams, I'd be on the cool team. It was a sure thing. Lud was *it*.

The sky was gray but it wasn't raining. As long as it isn't raining, we have P.E. outside. Mrs. Duncan, the P.E. teacher, loves laps. Some of the girls were already doing their laps. Mrs. Duncan was so busy yelling at kids and blowing her whistle that she didn't notice my new, cool image.

We did laps and more laps, and I was glad I'd used half the jar of Spike Stuff. My hair didn't move at all. Then we divided into teams for kick ball. Jason Miller was Team A captain. He picked Eddie immediately. Jennifer Davis was the captain for Team B. I was sure with my new image I would be one of the first to be chosen, but then Eddie called me Stegosaurus Head and told everyone I had a brain the size of a walnut, and as it ended up, Mrs. Duncan had to put me on

Team B, which was mostly girls. They didn't want me either.

Eddie and the other guys started calling us Team Barbie because of all the girls. Callie came up to me and tugged on my sleeve. She nodded in Eddie's direction. "I can't decide if he is an imbecile, a geek, or a cretin." Eddie was sticking his tongue out and jumping up and down. His eyes were crossed and he had a stupid look on his face, like *he* had a walnut for a brain.

"Definitely a cretin," I said, and then I yelled, "Eddie, you're a total cretin!" Eddie put his hand on his head like a rooster's comb and wiggled his fingers.

"Shut up, Stego-head," he yelled. "Boys rule!"

Team A was up first. They got nine home runs. Then it was our turn. Nine to zero. Eddie was pitching. The first two got on base. One girl fouled out. Finally it was my turn to kick. It had started to mist, not really rain, just a cool wetness somewhere between fog and the lowest form of drizzle.

Eddie rolled the ball to me and I kicked it hard, straight back at him. I ran for first base. Eddie dropped the ball and grabbed his crotch. He stayed doubled up like that for a while, until Mrs. Duncan asked if he needed a rest and he said no. Everyone was snickering. I was safe. Eddie was mad. Callie was next.

Callie is a little kid. For one thing, if she weren't a genius she'd be in fifth grade. Everyone knows what a bunch of shrimps fifth graders are. For another thing, Callie is short even for a fifth grader. She's more like fourth-grader size. So I was sure Eddie would cream her with the next pitch.

The Team A outfielders were chanting "Miss it, miss it, miss it," and I was getting ready to steal second base.

POW! Callie kicked the ball so hard it shot straight past second base and out toward the soccer field. She ran so fast I hardly had time to get off first base before she was there and screaming at me to move it. I took off. Team A went wild chasing the ball.

I tagged second base and ran for third. Someone caught the ball. Now the Team A kids were yelling "Throw it! Throw it!" Team B was yelling "Run! Run!" I passed third base so fast my foot slipped a little, but I didn't fall, and I was heading for home when my whole life fell apart.

The mist had turned to regular drizzle. My glasses were fogged. My face was soaked. So was my hair. I was just about to sprint into home when a big glob of Spike Stuff and green glitter slid down my face, crawled under my glasses and attacked my eyes. I was blind. Both of my eyes were full of glitter grit and burning from Spike Stuff. I grabbed for my eyes, knocked my glasses crooked, tried to catch them, lost my balance, and fell flat on my face, five feet from home plate.

But that's not all.

Callie was running so fast on those little legs of hers that she didn't have enough time to stop. BAM! The genius fell right on top of me. "Ow!" she cried, and then someone hit us hard with the rubber ball. We were out.

The Barbies started booing. Callie dripped blood all over my favorite Grateful Dead T-shirt. She was crying and holding her knee. I tried to wipe off the blood and smeared mud all over myself instead. There were kids pushing and shoving all around us.

"Look," said Eddie Grzinovich. "A nerd pile."
Everyone cracked up except Mrs. Duncan.

"Children, get out of the way!" she shouted. "Are
you all right, sweetheart?" she asked Callie. Mrs.
Duncan's a nice lady. Kind of a muscular grandma
with a whistle. Callie sniffed and nodded and one of
the other girls walked her to the nurse's office. I
watched her limp away and felt rotten. That T-shirt
cost me twelve bucks.

Mrs. Duncan didn't ask how I was. She just stood
there and stared. "For Pete's sake, Wiggie. What is
that green stuff all over your face?" she asked.

"Lud's blood," said Eddie, and everyone laughed.
Mrs. Duncan helped me up.

"I think you'd better go wash up, dear," she said,
and then we all went to change back into our regular clothes. Eddie led the guys in a chant all the way
back to the building.

Boys rule! Barbies lose! Boys rule! Barbies lose! I
could still hear them as I stuck my head under the
faucet in the boy's bathroom. I tried to use the squirty
pink hand soap for shampoo. It isn't shampoo.

The more I washed the more glitter spread around

and stuck to me. I had glitter on my face, in my ears, up my nose, all over my hands, and halfway to my elbows. I had to pick each piece off. I had red spots on my face every place I'd picked off a piece of glitter. My eyes were puffy and burning.

When I got back to class, Callie was sitting at her desk. I could see the bulge of a bandage under her right overall leg. "Sorry about your knee," I said. Callie shook her head and sighed.

"I should never have told you about getting a new image."

"But it's a great idea!" I said. "Anything is better than being a nerd. They called us *both* nerds! Don't you *hate* it?"

"I know I'm smart and I'm proud of it." Her dark eyes flashed. "When they me call names they're totally *stupid*!" She jerked her little body sideways in a defiant gesture and banged her hand down on the desk.

"Well, I'm not proud of it," I said. I didn't want to be called names, not for being smart, not for having a smart mom. It made *me* feel stupid when they called me a nerd.

"Being a nerd is better than being a Stegosaurus Head." said Callie.

"Lud was a rotten idea," I said, picking a piece of glitter off the back of my hand.

"I think you'd better quit acting so dorky," said Callie. "Act natural." Mr. Bell pulled down the map of South America. Callie turned and fished a box of colored pencils out of her desk.

Dorky? I thought as I got out my colored pencils and drew an oil well just off the coast of Venezuela. *Is that what she thinks? Is that what everyone thinks?* I bit the end of my pencil so hard a flake of paint stuck on my tongue. *Natural. Natural, natural, natural.* The word repeated itself in my head like a weird chant. *Act natural.*

So, what *is* natural, exactly?

I wasn't sure. All I knew was, I needed to give this new image thing a whole lot more thought.

Chapter Six

I did my chalkboard duty without running into Eddie. It's a good thing, too. I might have been tempted to clean erasers on his face. It quit raining and the sun came out just before I left for home, so I took the long way. Walking gave me time to think about my image. It gave me time to think about acting natural. It gave me time to pick glitter.

I dug in my ears until they burned, until I couldn't feel a single sharp piece of green glitter. Then I started on my arms. As soon as I turned down the Baker Street alley, when I was sure no one could see, I planned to take care of the glitter up my nose.

There was this one especially bad glob of glitter stuck in the hair on my left arm. I was picking it and walking and thinking about how I would boycott Spike Stuff for the rest of my life when BAM! I ran smack into Callie for the second time that day.

"Hey!" she said. "Are you trying to kill me?" Her voice sounded mad but I could tell she wasn't. She was smiling.

"Sorry," I said, picking another stubborn piece of glitter off my arm and flicking it off like it was nothing.

"Glitter problems?" asked Callie.

"Yeah," I said. "It's even up my nose." Callie giggled. I grinned. I guess it is pretty funny to have glitter up your nose.

"I'm on my way to my grandma's," said Callie. "I didn't know you lived around here."

"I don't," I said. "I had to stay after school." I looked around to make sure no one could see us together. Walking with a girl is deadly in sixth grade. "And I'm taking the long way."

"So you can pick the glitter out of your nose in private?"

"Something like that." I sniffed. There was a piece up there that really tickled.

We walked for about half a block. I couldn't think of anything to say. Someone was going to see us together for sure. Callie was limping. "Does your leg hurt a lot?" I asked finally.

"Not too bad."

"I didn't mean to cream you."

"I know," said Callie.

I wished she'd go away, even though she is a nice kid. If anyone caught us together, I'd never live it down. Girls can ruin a guy's life in an instant. At Seventh Street the tension was too much. And my nose was burning.

"Well, uh, this is where I turn," I said. "See you later." I was just about to take off running when Callie asked a question I didn't want to hear.

"Wiggie, how come you hate being smart so much?"

"I don't hate being smart," I said, but it was a lie.

I hated being different than other kids. I hated being called a nerd.

"Could have fooled me," said Callie. She crossed her arms across her chest and frowned. "So tell me what bizarre character you are going to be tomorrow so I can recognize you." That's it. She was starting to get under my skin.

"If your mom were the *Jump Into Science* teacher and all the kids made fun of you and drew pictures of you, you'd want a new image too. So lay off me," I said.

"If my mom were a TV scientist, I'd be proud," she said. I turned to walk away. The last thing I needed was a pride lecture from a girl.

"Check this out, Mr. Smart Guy Wiggie," Callie called after me. I sighed and turned around.

"What now?"

She dug into the pocket of her overalls and took out a folded-up piece of paper. It was folded so many times it was only about three inches long. She unfolded it carefully. It had pocket fuzz all over it.

"Here," she said. "You think you're the only one.

Well, you're wrong." I looked around to see if anyone was watching. Then I leaned over and looked at the paper. It was a drawing. At the top it said CALLIE. It was so bad, so mean, that it made THE CLASS NERD look like a poster from *Mister Rogers' Neighborhood.*

The picture of Callie was nasty. The page was covered with words I'd get grounded for a year for using, even if I whispered them. It was worse than a nerd picture. Way worse. It made me mad.

I let out a long whistle. "Who did this?"

"Girls in my other class."

"So why do you carry it around? I would have ripped it into a thousand pieces. That's what I did with THE CLASS NERD."

Callie looked at the picture for a long time. If it were a picture of me I'd be yelling and looking for someone to hit. Callie looked me in the eye.

"So I'll remember never to be like the girls who made it."

"Fat chance of that," I said, surprising myself. Callie smiled.

"I was furious," said Callie. "I wanted to get back

at those mean girls. I showed the picture to my grandma that same day. She said, 'Callie, this picture is all the things you're *not*. I'd hang on to it if I were you. For a reminder.' Then she said, 'Concentrate on the good people in life so you won't turn sour yourself.' So some other girls and I started a club. Anyone who wants to can be in it, if she's a girl I mean."

A girls' club? I thought. They probably compared Barbie collections and traded makeup tips.

"My grandma says if you fill up your heart with hate you won't have room for anything else. Get it?"

"Yeah, yeah, I get it." This was starting to sound like a Kindness and Goodness lecture. "I don't hate anyone," I said. I thought about that snake Eddie, how I'd like to grind his face into the dirt sometime, or better yet, into a fresh Foofie pile. OK. It was close to hate. And it did burn. Kindness and Goodness were the last things on my mind.

"If you hate being a smart kid, and keep trying to hide it from everybody, who do you hate really?" Callie squinched her eyes and pushed out her lips and looked right up at me. I picked glitter off one thumb.

I picked glitter off my elbow. I didn't answer.

"I'm not that stupid drawing," said Callie quietly. "And you aren't a nerd."

I wished I could believe her. It was no use. My whole family was nerdy. It was a fact. It was genetic and I felt trapped. It's not like I'm the only smart kid in the world, but the combination of being smart *and* having a TV scientist mom who talks about bowels had pushed me over the edge. I'd escaped being labeled for a long time. Now suddenly people pointed it out every day. Nerd. People like Billy, who used to be my friend. All I wanted was to be a regular kid. All I wanted was to be cool and have friends again, like before Mom became Mrs. Science.

"Hey! Look at the love couple!"

It was Eddie.

And Billy. And some other guys from school. Where had they come from? I stepped back from Callie. In two seconds they had us surrounded.

"So, is the little genius a good kisser?" asked Eddie. "Ooooh, nice outfit, Callie." He looked Callie up and down. He puckered up and made smooching noises. "Come on, nerds. Let's see some Nerd Love in action." Callie started to walk away.

"I'm leaving," she said, but her voice sounded quaky. Eddie grabbed her arm.

"Stay here, Brainiac," he said. "I want to see you kiss the Nerd."

"Shut up, Eddie," I said. "Let her go." I swallowed hard. My fist tightened into a ball.

"We just want to see you give her a little teensy smoochie." Eddie laughed. He started making kissing noises. So did the other boys. Billy too. Callie clenched her teeth. Tears welled up in her eyes. "A *French* kiss," Eddie said, and stuck out his tongue like a lizard. The other guys laughed. "All nerds know French."

"Get lost, you guys," My heart was beating in my throat. I was breathing hard through my nose, like a bull ready to charge. Eddie grinned and winked at me. I wanted to kick him. I wanted to kick Billy too, hard. Right in the shin. How could he hang out with such a creep? Eddie and the guys moved closer. I maneuvered for the best shot.

Just then, my nose exploded.

AH-choooo!

Liquid green glitter snot sprayed all over Callie's white sweater.

All I could do was stare. I should have said I was sorry right then and there but nothing came out. I was speechless. I was shocked. Here I was, ready to flatten Eddie, and out of my own nose comes this bomb. It was the stupidest, grossest thing I'd ever done.

I think Eddie started laughing first.

I couldn't bear to look at Callie. I stared down at my shoes. I wiped my nose with the back of my hand. Eddie was laughing hard. Billy and the others were laughing too. My mouth twitched. I bit my lip. I bit my cheek. I wiped my nose and opened my mouth to apologize but what came out was not words. I couldn't believe it. I had no control.

I started to laugh.

Chapter Seven

I didn't even laugh that long, just a big hoot and a couple of loud ha-has. I couldn't help it. It was automatic because of the green glitter boogers. Well, that and the fact that all of a sudden I'd realized they weren't laughing at *me*, not exactly. They were laughing at the sneeze. It was like I'd told a joke that cracked them up. Sneezing on Callie *was* funny in a way. It was also the lowest, rudest, most disgusting thing I've ever done to another person. Eddie doubled over. He howled and stomped the ground with one foot. Of course, Callie ran off crying.

Eddie was still hooting and snorting when I called

after her. "Hey! I'm really sorry! It was an accident!" She didn't turn around, just kept running, until she turned down an alley and was out of sight.

"That was a good one, Wiggie," said Eddie. "Boys rule." He whacked me on the back. Billy Lopez held up one hand and we did a high-five.

"Two points, man."

Eddie stopped laughing long enough to catch his breath. "There . . . were . . . sparkle boogers . . . everywhere!" His words came out between big funny gasps of laughter. I felt my ears turn red with embarrassed pleasure. I felt my face stretch tight in a grin. I mostly despise Eddie's guts, but it was nice not to be the joke. Finally they weren't treating me like a nerd.

"Hmmmm," said Eddie and looked in my ear. "I wonder if any of your brains came out when you sneezed." My grin disappeared.

"Doesn't matter," said Billy. He shoved me hard. "Nerds have extra brains in their butt, right, Wiggie?" The other guys laughed.

"See you later, Einstein," said Eddie. They turned and headed down the sidewalk in a tight group, like a school of piranhas looking for something new to rip apart. I sneezed again, and ran all the way home.

Foofie was sleeping up against the screen door. I had to shove him out of the way with my foot to get in. I shoved hard and he yipped. He's such a lazy, useless dog. He's also a big weenie. I hadn't shoved him *that* hard.

Of course Wolfie would have to be sitting at the kitchen table with a fat tablet of paper doing math. What else? Mom showed him some algebra and he does it for fun. Just once I wished I could come home and find him glued to the TV playing Komet Killers or Megatroid Madness, like any normal second grader from a normal Nintendo home.

"Mom showed me how to find a square root without the calculator," Wolfie said through his teeth. A pencil stub was jammed between his lips like a yellow cigarette. "Wanna see?" He looked up at me and frowned. "How come you're all sparkly?"

"Just shut up, Einstein face," I said. I didn't stop to see what he'd say. I didn't stop at the fridge. I didn't stop until my book bag, Foofie's stinking collar, and my bloody, muddy, glitter-infested Grateful Dead T-shirt were heaped on the floor and I was flopped face-down on the bed.

I have this way of lying on the bed with my face smashed into the pillow. Actually, just the top part of my face is smashed into the pillow or I'd smother. I scrunch down so my nose and mouth are below the bottom of the pillow so I can breathe. Then I stick another pillow over the back of my head and it's like I'm in my own little cave. I don't remember when I started doing it, but Mom says it was right after Dad died. It's a good way to hang out when I want to be alone. Nothing to look at, nothing to hear except my own pulse, whooshing in my ears.

I lay there for a long time. Was there no escaping this curse? If everyone thought I was such a nerd now, would I be a nerd for life? Like my mom with her rubber-glove smell? Like my dad? For a few seconds I'd been back to normal, just one of the guys. Billy even high-fived me like before when we were buddies. Then, BOOM! They were cutting on me worse than before. Now I was not only a nerd, I was a jerk for sneezing on Callie and laughing about it.

The one person who thought it was cool that I have a brain, and I'd emptied my nose on her.

I squeezed my eyes shut even tighter, pressing them into my pillow. I saw my dad's face, like in a photograph, smiling at me with those crooked teeth of his and those black horn-rimmed glasses he always wore. He was skinny, and his Adam's apple stuck out. I remember watching it go up and down as he talked. Remembering him made my eyes and my nose burn. I never knew Dad was a nerd back then, back when I was seven. Back then, he was just my dad and he was the bravest, coolest, smartest guy in the world. Would I ever stop missing him?

Someone knocked. Even through my pillows I could hear it. "Yeah?" I said. My voice kind of croaked.

"You okay, Wiggie?" It was Mom. "Wolfie said you were acting upset."

"I'm okay," I said.

"You sure?"

"Yeah." I listened until I heard her footsteps on the stairs. Then I buried my face in my pillow and cried, like a big fat wimpy baby.

Trying to change my image wasn't working. Ludwig and Lud were stupid ideas. What an idiot I'd been. I was going about this image thing all wrong. What I wanted was to blend in, go unnoticed. All I'd done so far was draw a lot of attention to myself, and it wasn't turning out to be the kind of attention I really wanted.

I wiped my eyes on my pillow and flipped it over so no one would see the wet spot. Then I rolled over onto my back and took a deep breath. I must have sucked in a piece of glitter, because suddenly I was coughing my brains out.

Downstairs, the phone rang. I stopped coughing just as my mom picked it up and said hello. I went over to the door and listened. What if it was Callie's mom? That's all I needed.

"Oh, hi Mr. Bell," I heard Mom say. Uh-oh. I wasn't out of the woods yet. What if Callie's mom had called Mrs. Jefferson? What if the General had called Mr. Bell and told him to call my mom? I listened. There were long pauses while Mom listened. She said a couple of things I couldn't hear through the door. There was another long pause. I had to hear what they were talking about. I had to know if I was doomed.

"Me too," said Mom. "It'll probably be quite chilly." They talked like that for a while, stupid stuff like the weather and what trees would have yellow and red leaves. Science stuff. I was just about to go back and lie down when I smelled a gross burning smell. I opened my door a little wider and sniffed. It was coming from downstairs. Mom smelled it too.

"Oh, my gosh," she said into the phone. "I totally forgot about the rice. *Take the rice off the stove, Wolfie!*" she yelled. To the phone she said, "Sorry about that. Looks like I just burned dinner." There was a pause, then Mom said, "Oh, nothing special. Just a simple Indonesian dish called *nasi goreng,*" and then she said something I couldn't hear, and then she said good-bye and hung up the phone.

"What stinks?" I yelled down.

"Burnt rice, dear," said Mom. I hopped down the stairs three at a time. There was my mom, staring at the wall phone with a puzzled look on her face.

"Who was it?" I asked, like the innocent and curious child that I am.

"It was Mr. Bell," said Mom. "Some details on the field trip. Can you believe he actually knew what *nasi goreng* is?" She hurried off to the kitchen.

Nasi goreng? Naus-eous is more like it. Actually, I was feeling quite nauseated right then. The field trip had completely slipped my mind again. Why did I keep forgetting it? I must have been blocking it out unconsciously, like war veterans do when the pain of remembering is too much. The mental images of Mrs. Science on the bus and kids snickering at me was definitely giving me a pain. That and the thought of *nasi goreng*.

I shuffled into the kitchen in the worst mood of my life. The rice had boiled over and white frothy gunk was everywhere, baked onto the stove and cooked all over the pan. The smell was hideous. I dug the crumpled permission slip out of my pocket and tossed it on the table for Mom to sign. Maybe if it looked enough like trash she'd throw it away. Wolfie was still finding square roots. Foofie was snoring. Eating Mom's latest toxic waste spill was the last thing on my mind.

I added up my miseries in my head. They sounded like headlines. SHOE ANNIHILATES BOY'S NOSE. BARBIES LOSE 9–2, SPIKE STUFF BLAMED. SNOT EXPLOSION OF THE CENTURY. COMING SOON: FIELD TRIP TRAUMA.

I jerked open the fridge, mostly out of habit. Nothing looked good. I slammed it shut and leaned against the door. It was only Wednesday, and I was heading downhill fast.

Chapter Eight

Since I didn't have plans for any more new images, I slept in the next morning. Wolfie woke me up when he yelled, "You're gonna be late for school!" and threw something hard at my feet. I kicked it onto the floor and saw it was a Ken doll. It was dressed in a long white coat with a tiny pocket patch that said Dr. Ken. At our house, even Ken is scientific.

I dressed in regular clothes and crawled down to the kitchen. Foofie was waiting by the table, begging silently with his droopy eyes. I grabbed a Cheerio out of Wolfie's bowl and flicked it to the floor. Foofie licked it up. Mom had taped the permission slip to my lunch bag and left it in the middle of the table. The sight of it almost made me lose my appetite. Almost, but not quite. I scarfed down six toaster waffles and a couple of glasses of OJ, and Wolfie and I were out the door by 7:45 sharp.

While Wolfie chattered at me about computer lab class, I rehearsed how I would apologize to Callie.

"Do you think Mr. Riccardi would let me do some programming if I asked?" said Wolfie. "I know AppleScript already."

"Yeah, sure, Wolf, I'm sure he will." I said it automatically. I was dreading seeing Callie. I mean, if someone sneezed like that on me and laughed about it, I'd be furious. In my head I was thinking, *She's going to hate me forever.*

OK, I could write her a note.

Nah, people would think we're in love.

OK, I could just say it quick, right before class, in the hall. "I'm *totally* sorry . . ."

Nah, sounds too much like begging.

Or I could wait until recess, or lunch, and apologize then. All those toaster waffles had made a serious ball in my stomach. I couldn't stop thinking about Callie. I hated thinking about what I'd done. I hated thinking how much she must hate me for being such a jerk. I kept trying to convince myself that it didn't matter, that she was just a girl, and who cares what girls think anyway?

OK. I could wait until the bell rings, sit down, whisper it while we're sitting in our desks.

Nah.

I dropped Wolfie off at his class and hurried down the hall to my own locker. Eddie and Billy were just going into the classroom. "Hey, it's the walking sneeze machine," said Eddie.

"Uh-uh-uh-CHOO!" said Billy. Eddie laughed and made his finger into a gun and pointed at me.

"Fire one!" said Eddie. He plugged one nostril with his finger. Then he switched to the other side. "Fire two!"

I turned away and concentrated on hanging up my jacket. I clenched my teeth until they hurt. I heard Eddie's voice. "Hey, Wigman. I hear you know how to play basketball."

"Yeah," I said.

"Wanna play three on three after lunch?" I looked

up to see both guys smiling at me. It wasn't mean smiling, either. I hesitated, but not for long.

"Sure," I said. A humongous smile started deep in my chest and pushed up until it burst out on my face.

"Me and Chili need another guy. Boo-boo twisted his foot last night." Chili is Eddie's name for Billy. Boo-boo is what he calls Bo Serich. And now I was Wigman. Not Nerd, not Einstein, not Bowel Boy.

"Sounds good," I said. My heart was pounding. Coolness, I told myself. Coolness is what counts. Give me half a chance and I can be as cool as anyone, even Eddie Grzinovich. I slammed my locker shut. Eddie and Billy actually waited for me. They were wearing their Seahawks jackets. I wished I had one too.

Billy did a turn-around jump shot with a candy wrapper, right into Mr. Bell's trash can. Eddie yelled, "Two points!" Mr. Bell frowned and told us to sit down. Billy and I slapped high-fives. We were friends again.

Callie hurried past us and took her seat. Oh yeah, I thought. Her.

I sat down just as the bell rang. I was still feeling

incredibly cool. And incredibly stupid. I looked out of the corner of my eye at Callie. She'd turned in her chair so her back was to me. She was mad. I could tell. It was now or never.

"Pssst." No response. "Hey, Callie."

We stood for the Pledge of Allegiance. Callie didn't look at me. When she sat back down, her note-book slid off the desk and fell with a smack on the floor. I scooped it up and handed it to her, but she didn't look at me or say thanks. Mr. Bell asked for our math homework from the day before. Then he asked if anyone else had a permission slip to turn in. I raised my hand and said I'd give it to him at lunch. He said that was OK. "What do you want me to call you today?" he asked.

"Just Wiggie," I said.

"He's the Wigman," said Eddie in a loud voice. Everyone laughed. Billy held one finger under his nose and then faked a huge sneeze. Mr. Bell pushed his glasses up on his nose.

"You boys want to skip recess?" asked Mr. Bell. Eddie snorted and slumped down in his desk. I felt my face blaze. Eddie was such a troublemaker.

He didn't seem to give a rip if he made Mr. Bell mad.

Before everyone started saying I was a nerd, I was pretty close to being Teacher's Pet. Whenever I'd get a hundred on a really hard math test, Mr. Bell would whisper "Super job, Wiggie," when he gave back my paper. I like Mr. Bell a lot. He's smart and he's nice, even if he is sort of fat. Maybe Callie would be Teacher's Pet now. The thought made me a little sad.

I turned toward Callie and tried to get her attention. "Pssst." She took a BIC pen out of her book bag. She didn't look at me. "I'm sorry about yesterday," I said. Jackie Zim poked Callie in the back. Callie took the stack of math papers from Jackie, added her own, and passed the stack forward. Maybe she hadn't heard me.

"I said I'm sorry. Really. It was an accident." Finally Callie looked at me. Her big brown eyes were full of tears. One slipped down her cheek. She wiped it away with the back of her hand.

"I thought we could be friends," she said. "But you're nothing but a big stupid jerk, like your stupid jerk friends!" She stuck out her tongue at me. Then she turned away. I felt like a dog.

Nobody ever called me a stupid jerk before.

Mr. Bell made us do a lot of review and drilling that morning. First it was social studies. Then it was spelling. Then geography. Every time he called on Callie she got the answer right. She didn't even have to think. She just knew. I could tell Mr. Bell was proud of her. Once I heard Jackie Zim say, "She thinks she's so smart," in a snotty way, loud enough for a few of us to hear, quiet enough not to get in trouble. Out of the corner of my eye I saw Callie's face turn a rosy brown color. I felt rotten for her. I've blushed plenty in my lifetime and I hate it.

Every time Mr. Bell called on me I blew it. Largest ethnic group in the world? I said white. White isn't an ethnic group. The answer is Mandarin Chinese. Spell Antarctica? No problem. Except that like a moron I forgot the first *t*. The worst was when he asked for the capital of Guatemala. Instead of Guatemala City I said, "Acapulco?" The room exploded in laughter.

Mr. Bell was ticked. I could tell by the way he shook his head. He must have thought I was goofing off, but I wasn't, honest. Now that I think about it, I'd say he seemed more sad than anything. Seeing him look sad made me feel like a zero on top of being a stupid jerk. The worst part is, he probably wouldn't have believed me if I'd told him that for once I wasn't faking the wrong answers.

See, my brain that morning was like a junkyard of thoughts and feelings. On the one hand, I couldn't wait for lunch recess. I looked at the clock every six seconds. I hadn't played three on three with Billy since Eddie came. On the other hand, it was hard to forget the pain in Callie's eyes. It was hard not to feel her hurt radiating toward me from her desk. I was the world's biggest bozo. I was a stupid jerk! I was also on my way to being cool, finally. *Finally!* No wonder I couldn't think straight.

I forgot all about Callie during recess. Three on three was great. We played a girls team, the one Becky Luik is on. She's in Mrs. Anderson's class. She must be six feet tall, but we beat them anyway. I made a couple of shots right off and blocked a couple others. I faked a pass to Billy. Eddie caught on and made two points. I stole the ball once, passed it to Billy, and he made a shot. By the time we were done we were sweating like hogs. We won, 28–20. "Boys RULE!" we yelled about six times. The girls said they'd get us at the next recess. On the way back to class Eddie kept shoving me and saying he never knew straight-A boys could play ball so well.

"*Acapulco?*" said Billy in a perfect Spanish accent. He grinned and punched me in the arm. "That was a good one, Wiggie. Guess you're not *that* smart." Eddie laughed. I laughed too, but it was a fake laugh. Billy's comment stung. It shouldn't have, but it did.

Thursdays we have music. Usually we have Mrs. Lubeck, but that day there was a sub. He was a little old guy with eyebrows like black caterpillars and hairs sticking out of his ears. He said his name was Mr. Andraus. He told us at the beginning of music class that Mrs. Lubeck wanted us to practice on the risers. That meant we'd be in the auditorium for a change. I got out of my seat and headed for the door. Billy and Eddie caught up.

There's this Winter Festival Concert in December, and all three of the sixth-grade classes have to sing together. I guess Mrs. Lubeck figured we needed an early start, since it was only October. She knows us pretty well. Anyway, Mr. Andraus put Eddie way up on the third riser. He put Billy down on the first one. He put me in between. Callie ended up in the front with the other short kids. If Mr. Andraus had been Mrs. Lubeck, he would have put Billy and Eddie at opposite ends of the risers, but he was only a sub and didn't know any better. It was a perfect setup for disaster. Jennifer Davis spread her music out on the piano. Mr. Andraus signaled for her to start playing.

We were right in the middle of "Silver Bells" when Billy let one rip. It was an audible. It was also the biohazard of the century. My nose was the first one it hit. Girls started holding their nose. Guys started waving the air and gagging. By the time Mr. Andraus noticed the commotion, kids were coughing and choking. I'm sure I heard Callie say, "That's so disgusting." It was all a big show, something to do instead of sing. Nothing entertains like intestinal gas.

"Settle down over there, altos," said Mr. Andraus. He tapped his music stand with a pencil. Jennifer stopped playing. Everyone was talking at once.

"We can't breathe," said Eddie. "How are we supposed to sing?"

"Billy let one," said Jackie Zim.

"It wasn't me, man," said Billy. "I didn't fart." By the time he said "fart," everyone else had stopped talking, so it came out loud and clear. Mr. Andraus's caterpillar eyebrows shot up. His round face turned purple. I doubled over with laughter and in that very moment Eddie moved back a little, and I hit him in the head with my wide open mouth. My teeth whacked into his skull. Eddie swore.

"Hey, sorry, Eddie," I said. My front teeth were throbbing.

"Man, you got fangs," said Eddie, rubbing his head. "What are you, Dracula?"

I don't know what came over me just then. I don't know why I didn't keep my big mouth shut. "I vant to suck your blood!" I yelled. Eddie's eyes flew open in fake fear.

"Wigman's a vampire! He's after me!" Eddie yelled. Girls started screaming. That close to Halloween, vampires are a popular topic in the sixth grade.

"Quiet, boys and girls!" shouted Mr. Andraus. But it was too late. Suddenly all the boys were showing their teeth like vampires. All of the girls were squealing. Eddie held his arms out stiff and plunged down the risers like a zombie. We made a path so he could pass through. When he got to the bottom he turned around and took a bow. Mr. Andraus grabbed him. And Billy. And me.

There we were, back in the principal's office, back at the General's desk, me, Eddie, and now Billy. Busted because of a fart.

Mrs. Jefferson made us call our moms to tell them where we were and why, and how come we'd be doing two hours detention after school. She sat there and glared at us while we called. Billy had to go first. He dialed the number. After a couple of words he switched into Spanish. I don't understand Spanish, but I could hear Billy's mom screaming. Usually she's a real quiet lady. Mad Mom sounds the same in any language.

Eddie went next. His grandma answered the phone. Mad Grandma is almost as bad as Mad Mom.

I dialed my mom at the U. The lab secretary put

me through to Mom's office. "Hi, Mom," I said when she answered. I explained everything. Well, not *everything*, but the general idea. She didn't scream. She didn't yell. At first, I wasn't even sure she was listening. "Mom? Are you there?"

"Yes, Wiggie." Mom sighed into the phone.

"Are you mad?"

"No, I'm not mad," said Mom. "I'm just terribly, terribly disappointed. And I'm concerned about you. That's all." She sat there on the phone without saying anything else. I bit the inside of my cheek and felt like living scum. There was just no way to explain it to her, no way at all. There was no way to make her understand the craziness in my head, the wanting to be cool and wanting Mr. Bell to like me and wanting to have guy friends and wishing Callie wasn't mad at me. It was like I had a whole zoo of feelings inside. Now I was in serious trouble. Twice in one week I'd sat across from the General. But I didn't want to be in trouble. I just wanted to stop being a nerd. Why did Mom have to say she was disappointed? Screaming would have been a million times easier to take.

Mr. Bell didn't say a word when Eddie, Billy, and I returned to class after calling our moms. In fact, he ignored our existence for the rest of the day. He didn't call on me at all during math. I must have raised my hand a zillion times. I knew a bunch of the answers that other kids got wrong, too. I just never got the chance to prove it. By the end of the day I realized something that kind of freaked me out. Being ignored by Mr. Bell was almost, *almost* worse than being a nerd.

Chapter Nine

After school I did my detention with Eddie and Billy. At first I felt horrible. I've never been the kind of kid to get detention. Twice in one week was now my lifetime record. We had to clean chalkboards and empty trash cans.

At first Billy seemed pretty bummed out too, but then he and Eddie made a big game out of the detention jobs, wadding papers into balls and slam-dunking them into the bigger cans. Eddie told a bunch of funny stories of being on detention at his other school. He did all these teachers' voices until Billy and I were laughing our heads off. Pretty soon

I was slam-dunking the paper balls too. Eddie and Billy didn't seem to care about getting in trouble. I tried hard not to care either.

Some of the chalk erasers are these big long suckers. I got the idea of seeing who could balance one on his nose and walk the farthest. No grownups were around. Eddie and Billy and I lined up in the first-grade classroom, right up in the front where the teacher stands. We balanced erasers on our noses and I said, "One, two, three, GO!" We walked as fast as we could to the other end of the room, squeezing between the little first-grader desks. We were almost to the back of the class when Eddie tripped on a microscopic chair and fell over and we all lost our erasers. Mine flopped sideways and got chalk all over my left cheek. Billy's fell upward and gave him a yellow nose and a yellow streak in his black hair.

We were laughing so hard that at first we didn't see Mr. Bell standing in the doorway. "What's going on?" he said, and there we were, a pile of boys with chalk all over our faces. No one said a word. Mr. Bell's face did a bunch of jumpy twitches and turned beet red.

After a lecture that made me feel the size of an amoeba that lives in someone's bowels, we finished our jobs and headed home. I tried hard to keep up the goofing-off spirit of things, like Billy and Eddie did, but I couldn't get the image of Mr. Bell's angry face out of my mind.

"See you tomorrow, Wigman," said Billy when we were all done. "Field trips are a blast."

"Yeah," said Eddie. "We can go on the bus together, as long as you don't have to sit with your mama."

"I can sit where I want," I said, reminded once again of the impending doom field trip. Would Mom make me sit with her? Would she make me walk around with her? Would she make me help her collect specimens? If she did, was there any way to get out of it without hurting her feelings? I remembered that we had certain other things to discuss when I got home, such as my getting in trouble twice in the same week. What if all of a sudden she announced that I had to stay with her all day, so she could keep an eye on me? What if Mr. Bell called her and told her to keep me away from Eddie and Billy? Would he do that?

Me and Billy slapped five, and Eddie waved good-bye. I ran all the way home. Might as well get the yelling over with.

Mom was on the phone when I got there. All I heard was, "Thanks for calling, Mr. Bell." I tried sneaking up the stairs to my room, but my mom has radar ears. "Wiggie, I want to talk to you." I dumped my books on the stairs and sighed. Here it comes, I thought.

Actually, it wasn't that bad at first. We went into the kitchen and Mom stirred me up a big glass of chocolate milk. She gave me the basic I'm-worried-about-you speech, which included Mr. Bell telling her about my grades going down and about my hanging out with Eddie and Billy. "Mr. Bell says this Eddie character isn't exactly a model student," said Mom. "And what's going on with Billy? I thought he was such a nice boy." I shrugged.

"He *is* nice, Mom. And Eddie just goofs off a lot," I said. "Can't I even have friends?" OK, so maybe Eddie wasn't exactly an angel. That isn't news. But I didn't like my mom and Mr. Bell cutting on him.

"Of course you can have friends," said Mom. "But

make sure they don't influence you negatively."

You can probably figure out how the rest of that little lecture went. I got myself some more milk and added more chocolate. Mom kept talking. She was worried. Mr. Bell was worried. Peer pressure and peer influence, blah, blah, blah. The usual stuff. While she talked I daydreamed about playing basketball with the guys. It felt great to whip the girls' team. I thought about doing detention, about how even the punishment felt worth it. I wasn't a nerd anymore, at least not to Eddie and Billy, and it was all because of a sneeze. I made myself a third glass of chocolate milk.

I was thinking Mom had a lot of nerve lecturing me about Billy and Eddie. They weren't all bad. So what if they were showoffs? It's a free country, right? If they wanted to be friends, so did I. I'd just have to watch out and not get in any more trouble. Moms who lecture for a living tend to drone on and on. I needed to get outside and practice my turn-around jump shot. Out of the blue, Mom asked, "Do you remember Mrs. Daniels?"

"Sure," I said. I took a swig. Mrs. Daniels is the

secretary at the DNR, the Department of Natural Resources. Mom does work for them now and then, like when there's a tapeworm epidemic in the raccoon population. Mrs. Daniels has really cool white hair.

"Mrs. Daniels's granddaughter Callie was just skipped ahead to your class." The chocolate milk I was drinking suddenly turned into brown Jell-O. I gagged it down. Mom went on. "I guess she's exceptionally intelligent. Mrs. Daniels is very proud."

"I noticed there was a new girl," I said. My mouth had a sour taste. Milk does that.

"Anyway, Mrs. Daniels told me she's worried that the kids are picking on Callie. She said Callie came to her house in tears the other day because some kids were teasing her. You don't know anything about that, do you?"

I shook my head. Did Callie tell about the sneeze? Did Mom know? My stomach was way, way too full. No way could I play ball now. I needed to burp. I set down my glass and glanced sideways at Mom. She was staring at me through her thick glasses. "From what Mr. Bell tells me, Eddie is just the type to torment another child." She kept staring. I could feel her eyes burning a hole in the side of my head. "Isn't Eddie the same one who kicked you?"

"Give him a break, Mom," I said, wishing she would stop drilling me. "Eddie and Billy are just regular guys. Sometimes they joke around too much. Sometimes they hassle the girls." Eddie and Billy wanted to be friends. I was on their team and I'm no snitch. Besides, I'd said I was sorry to Callie. Was it my fault she wouldn't listen?

We didn't talk about it any more after that. Miraculously, Mom ordered two pineapple and pepperoni pizzas for dinner, but even though it's my favorite kind I could only manage to eat one piece. Mom asked if I was feeling all right. I told her I had a bunch of homework hanging over my head. I excused myself and went straight up to my room.

The homework part was a little white lie. The only homework I had to do was *in* my head, not hanging over it. I lay on my bed, staring at the ceiling and thinking about my life as a nerd. I thought about the first time Mom went on TV, how happy she'd been about it, how totally embarrassed I'd felt. I thought about that CLASS NERD picture of me with all the calculators and pens.

I thought about the day Callie came and how she knew mummies don't bleed. OK, I was impressed. I thought about her telling me to get a new image, what a great idea it had seemed; and then I thought about my two idiotic attempts.

I thought about Callie showing me that mean picture of herself, how much I liked talking to her, even if she was a girl, even though I'd dreaded getting caught with her, and then of course, everything that happened afterward.

Maybe after a while of hanging out with Eddie and Billy, everyone would forget about the whole nerd thing. Maybe Callie would even forget about me laughing at her. And even if she didn't, who cares? She was only a girl. Boys rule. Boys rule. *Boys rule.*

Don't they?

I sat up and punched my pillow. No matter what, I was done being a nerd. If I had to hang around with Eddie and Billy, too bad. Just hanging around with them wasn't going to turn me into some kind of delinquent. Tough and cool isn't the same as being a criminal.

Tough and cool. That's the opposite of being a nerd for sure! And it was the only way I'd survive that field trip. Billy and Eddie and I would hang out together all day. We'd be totally bored with the science stuff. We'd chew gum and shake our soda pops up so they'd geyser when we opened them, and afterward, we'd throw rocks at the empty cans. Everyone would see how I was just like any old regular non-scientific kid. *Yes!*

Boys rule.

I heard a soft knock on my door. "Yeah?" I said.

"It's me," said Wolfie. "Can I come in?"

"Go ahead," I said. The door opened and a little blond head peeked around from behind. Then Wolfie's beat-up one-eyed monkey puppet named Mr. Spock popped out from behind the door and nodded at me. It was Wolfie's favorite toy, next to his microscope. Tough and cool, I thought. Might as well start with Wolfie.

I set my face in a tough frown and tried to look

bored. The stuffed monkey waved its little paw at me. I bit the inside of my cheek.

"What do you want, Wolfie?" It was a pretty bored-sounding voice.

"I thought you might be lonely," said Wolfie in a squeaky high voice. "Can I come in?" Now Mr. Spock had his paws spread wide. Wolfie's glasses had slipped almost all the way down his nose. My toughness was weakening. My coolness was slipping away. I decided it was going to take some practice. I'd have a lot of practice on the field trip.

I grinned at my little brother and his ragged old monkey. He grinned back, looking exactly like a vampire with his two front teeth gone. He tossed the puppet onto the bed and stepped into my room. In his other hand, Wolfie had a pizza box. Foofie was sniffing it from behind.

"Here's the extra pizza, in case you get hungry." He brought it over and sat on the edge of the bed. I took the box from him and opened it up. "Want some?" asked Wolfie. I had the urge to hug that little punk, nerdy as he was. Luckily, the smell of the pizza hit my nose and I remembered I was dying of starvation before I could do something as wimpy as hug my brother.

Wolfie sat and watched me finish the pizza. When I was done I closed up the box and belched. It was a huge one, a nine on a scale from one to ten.

"I wish I could burp like you," said Wolfie. The awe in his voice was unmistakable. So for the next half hour I showed him how to suck in air and then how to belch it out in an extra loud way. I showed him how to do baby burps and humongous burps and burp talking. Pretty soon Wolfie was doing it. Mom was not going to like this. I belched and Wolfie belched and we laughed so hard we rolled off the bed. Mr. Spock got flattened underneath us, but he didn't complain.

All of a sudden Wolfie grabbed me around the head and squeezed. "You're the best brother, Wiggie." A very mushy and uncool feeling grabbed my throat, and it wasn't a burp. I swallowed. Wolfie pulled away and looked at me. His face was totally serious. "Maybe we could borrow Mom's camera and make a documentary video of us burping," he said. "You know, of all the ways to do it." That did it. Even when he was belching he was thinking of ways to make it educational.

I tickled Wolfie until he howled. Finally he broke away laughing, and so I chased him all the way down the hall to his room. When I got back to my own room I was breathing hard. I scooped Mr. Spock up off the floor and patted him on the head. Good thing Eddie didn't see me playing with my little brother. He probably beat on his.

It was going to take some practice to be cool all the time, at least all the time I was at school, but I knew I could do it. I'd need a few adjustments to my image, but nothing like before. Thinking about it got me plenty excited. I made a list of all the stuff I needed to take on the field trip. I hesitated when I got to the last thing. Wolfie had given me the idea and it was a great one. I almost didn't write it down. Finally I clenched my teeth and added it to my list.

Take video camera.

Mom would never find out.

Chapter Ten

I should have known Friday started out too good to be true. Mom announced at breakfast that she would be taking the car instead of riding the bus with the rest of us. I could hardly believe my ears. While I happily inhaled my third bowl of chocolate Malt-O-Meal she explained that she had some science club meeting to go to, and that she'd meet the class up at the ranger station in Longview. I tried to act disappointed. I did. Really. "Too bad, Mom," I said in a sad voice.

Just then, Wolfie let out a huge belch. I stayed cool, biting the inside of my cheek so I wouldn't sputter Malt-O-Meal everywhere. Mom gave Wolfie a manners lecture.

Mom took off right after breakfast and that was my signal to get ready. I had a new image to uphold and I was pumped. Subtle, I kept telling myself. My new image had to be subtle and natural. First, I took off my glasses. I had to squint to see, but big deal. I changed out of my pajamas and put on Levi's and my best Elvis T-shirt. Over that I put on my Seahawks sweatshirt and pulled and yanked the sleeves until they hung just past my hands. Too-long sleeves look cool, I thought. Lots of kids wear them that way. Even if I didn't have an official NFL jacket like Eddie and Billy, at least I could wear my sweatshirt.

I dug the jar of Spike Stuff out of the trash and put a little on my hair, just enough to get the front part to stick up like Billy's does. Then I ran down the hall to my room and found my tube of Super Glue in the bottom of my junk drawer. I pulled a black BIC pen out of my backpack and took the little plug out of the end. With my pocket knife I cut off the part that sticks into the pen so I had this perfect black plastic dot left, then I took it to the bathroom and glued it on my left earlobe. So what if there's this warning on the tube about getting Super Glue on your skin? In a pinch, a guy has to use what's handy. I squinted at myself in the mirror and grinned. I was the essence of natural coolness.

Next I got out my list and packed all the stuff I needed in my backpack, including the video camera. I fed Foofie and told him not to sleep all day, then Wolfie and I left for school. I was in the mood to run, but you don't want to look too eager when you're acting cool. Also, I didn't want that camera bouncing around. It was bad enough using it without asking. If anything happened to it, I'd be dead meat. I settled for a slow jog, with Wolfie griping the whole way for me to slow down. When we got to school, the long yellow field trip bus was idling outside the building.

Eddie and Billy were already on the bus. They waved at me from the back window. "We saved you a seat, Wigman," shouted Eddie. We slapped fives when I got back to them. Eddie whistled when he saw my ear. "Nice touch," he said, and punched my shoulder. Did they notice I wasn't wearing my glasses? I didn't say a word, and I had to bite the insides of my cheeks to keep from grinning like an idiot. I swung around coolly and sat down. I laid my backpack carefully on the seat.

"You don't have to sit with your mom, do you, Wiggie?" asked Billy.

"No," I said. "She isn't taking the bus," I said. Other kids got on, girls sitting with girls, boys sitting with boys. I figured Callie was probably up there near the front. I couldn't see that well, so I wasn't sure. Not like I cared where she sat, now that she hated my guts. Mr. Bell got on last, and gave the standard talk about riding on the bus. Billy and Eddie and I slumped down in our seat and Eddie made faces while he spoke. He polished the top of his head with one hand like he was bald. Mr. Bell is really a nice teacher. It bugged me that Eddie was making fun of him, but then all of a sudden Billy stuck his backpack under his shirt to look fat and I lost control. I had to clamp my hand over my mouth so I wouldn't laugh out loud.

Mount Rainier National Park is an hour and a half away. A bunch of girls sang stupid Girl Scout songs. Right in the middle of "John Jacob Jingleheimer Schmidt," at the quiet part where everyone is supposed to be singing silently, Billy shouted out, "Bah-bah-BAMBA," and instantly all the boys were singing "Bah-bah-BAMBA." Billy and I sang all the Spanish words to "La Bamba" while everyone else sang "Bah-bah-BAMBA" until Mr. Bell made us settle down. I could tell Eddie was impressed that Billy and I knew Spanish. "La Bamba" was way more fun than "John Jacob Jingleheimer Schmidt."

Only one kid puked on the trip. Jamie Keller. Mr. Bell had remembered to bring barf bags and Jamie asked for one in time. Still, I felt sorry for Jamie. She used to be pretty popular, but throwing up in public can instantly erase a person's popularity. The girl that was with her sat in another seat, probably because of the smell. I don't blame her.

About halfway to the park I looked around to see where Callie had ended up. I squinted hard and checked out every head on that bus and discovered that she wasn't on the bus. I felt a surge of total relief. Maybe she was sick or something. At least she wouldn't be around to stick her tongue out at me and call me a stupid jerk.

We got to the park at nine-thirty. From my window I could see our car parked in front of the ranger station. Mom was nowhere in sight. I put on my backpack and hurried off the bus.

It was cold outside. I wished I'd worn my hooded jacket instead of the Seahawks sweatshirt, but Eddie and Billy were bareheaded too, so I decided it was no big deal even though my ears were freezing. Mr. Bell stood on the top step of the ranger station porch. He was wearing earmuffs. I actually envied him, but just a little. Without my glasses he looked like a boiled egg with red powder puffs for ears.

All the kids were gathered at the bottom of the steps. We stood at the back of the group. The door to the ranger station opened and out came my mom. Out came Callie and three other girls from our class. All of a sudden I realized I hadn't seen any of them on the bus. Bess Jules. Gillian Wong. Elise Emmenthal. They were all quiet girls, the kind that aren't popular or nerds, just there.

"I'd like to introduce Dr. Carter," said Mr. Bell. He smiled and rocked forward on his toes. I made myself slightly shorter. "Wiggie Carter's mom." Eddie elbowed me in the ribs.

"Where's her white coat?" he asked.

"She only wears it in the lab or on TV," I said. Even without my glasses I could see Mom was dressed for fieldwork. Jeans, warm shirt and sweater, L.L. Bean parka, leather Nike hiking shoes. She had her backpack slung over one shoulder. She also had on her hideous work glasses, the ones with the indestructible black plastic frames. I was glad I'd left my glasses at home.

"Hi, kids," said Mom, in that fakey Mrs. Science way. She pushed her industrial glasses up. They don't fit as well as her other ones. "Sorry I couldn't ride up on the bus with you, but I had a special request from the Girls' Science Club." She put one arm around Callie and smiled.

"What Girls' Science Club?" asked Eddie. I

shrugged. "How come they got a science club?"

So that was the club Callie was talking about. Not a Barbie doll club. A science club. I should have figured.

"Callie and the other girls asked me if we could ride up here to the park together," said Mom. "On the way we talked about a very interesting idea." *That* was the meeting Mom had to go to? I swallowed. Had Callie told Mom about the megasneeze? My mom, the Ph.D. and Manners Queen, would not take too kindly to me sneezing all over another kid and then laughing about it. I felt sweat beading on my upper lip, which is strange because I was shivering. Mom kept talking.

"The girls in the science club suggested I perform a dissection. They're learning about taxidermy, and thought the rest of the class might be interested."

"What's faxidermy?" asked Eddie.

"*Tax*idermy," I corrected. Is that why Callie knew about mummies being desiccated?

"That's when dead stuff is stuffed, Eddie," said Billy. "Shut up so I can hear." Billy punched him in the arm. Eddie shoved Billy and took a playful swing at his head, but Billy ducked in time. Mr. Bell looked in our direction and frowned. I blended in with the crowd.

"The rangers here have some frozen specimens and have agreed to let us have a chipmunk or maybe a marmot. So after lunch we'll have a little anatomy lesson. The girls will be assisting me." By this time I had made myself a little less than three feet tall. Who ever heard of a mom who cuts up Chip 'n' Dale for a good time?

"That's no fair that the girls get to help," said Eddie, loud enough for everyone to hear. Mr. Bell frowned over at us. I stared at Eddie. Eddie shut up, but the look on his face was mad. Now Mom was talking about taking a nature walk.

". . . and the group that finds the single most interesting evidence of animal life on the nature trail will be guests on the *Jump Into Science* show!" She was really grinning now. I wanted to die. Kids were murmuring and ooooohing and aaaahhing. A couple of them turned around and pointed at me. My ears burned. I shrunk another two inches. I didn't want everyone looking at me because of *her*.

Why couldn't my mom be like other moms? Other

moms didn't come on field trips and cut up small animals. Other moms didn't do educational TV shows. Other moms wore decent-looking glasses in public.

Finally Mom stopped talking and grinning and we broke up into smaller groups and got ready to go. The Nature Trail is really long. It goes all over the place. It would be easy to get away from the crowd. I stuck with Eddie and Billy. Mom told everyone to look for evidence of what animals might be eating (like pinecones torn apart) and for places where beavers might have gnawed or where bears might have sharpened their claws. When she mentioned bears, a couple of girls squealed.

Mom reminded everyone not to disturb any plants or trees. Finally, she mentioned the unmentionable. She said we can learn a lot about an animal from examining its droppings. I cringed. No one laughed, though a couple of kids said, "Gross." Mr. Bell had his eagle eye on us all.

Next, Mom passed out plastic bags for our collections. When she got to me, she said, "Why didn't you wear your warm jacket, honey?" Billy shoved me. I shrugged and didn't look at her.

Mr. Bell put Jennifer Davis and Arlee Wurtzbauer with us. "Oh, no!" yelled Eddie. "Ghouls!" Billy made a gagging sound. The girls sneered at us, like we were some kind of lower life form.

Mr. Bell said we could go anywhere in the meadow area, but we had to stay on the trail and we had to stay in groups. Eddie and Billy looked at each other. Then they looked at me. The three of us looked at the girls in our group. As soon as no one was looking, we took off running and left the girls in the dust. The fun was about to begin.

Chapter Eleven

"So, what do you guys want to do?" I asked as soon as the girls were out of sight. I shoved my plastic bag in my jeans pocket. My heart was racing. I was ready to goof off, to act cool, to hang out with these guys. I patted the video camera in my backpack. These guys wouldn't want to collect animal droppings. I was sure of that.

"I always bring stuff to do on a field trip," said Eddie. He looked at Billy in a knowing way and pointed to his back pocket. It was bulging. Probably candy.

"Me too," said Billy. "'Cuz there's no teachers around to hassle us." They slapped five.

"I've got a bunch of Cheetos in my backpack," I said. "And three cans of root beer." Food is a hit at any hour, I thought, but it turned out I was wrong.

"Forget about the food, Wigman," said Eddie. "We got a ton of work to do."

"Yeah," said Billy. "We gotta win this contest."

"Boys rule," said Eddie.

"You mean collecting stuff?" I asked, completely stunned by this news. The last thing I'd expected was to actually go along with what the rest of the class was doing. I'd come with plans to goof off, not traipse around the woods filling plastic bags with squirrel fur. They wanted to be in on the contest? Back before Eddie came, Billy might have been interested in this kind of stuff. I mean, he did trade me for that frog. But after the way he'd been acting lately, I couldn't believe it. My mouth hung open in amazement. So much for coolness.

"Duh, Wigman," said Eddie. "Your mom said the winners get to go on TV."

"You *want* to go on *Jump Into Science*?" I asked. "I thought you guys hated that show."

"We don't want a bunch of girls to beat us," said Eddie. "It wouldn't look good. If anyone goes on TV it should be us. Boys win everything." Billy grinned and nodded. They were forgetting about spelling contests, math contests, social studies contests, subjects the girls creamed the guys in on a regular basis. I decided not to point that out.

"Hey," said Eddie. "How come you never told us those girls had a science club with your mom? How come she's showing them how to dissect animals and not us?"

"You can watch the dissection if you want," I said.

"Yeah, but the girls get to help her," said Eddie.

"Big deal," I said. All my plans for a great day were fizzling like a bunch of dud fireworks.

"Hey," said Eddie. "Did you and your girlfriend, the Brain, think this up?"

"Think what up?" I asked. I was feeling confused. Why all this interest in science and my mom and those girls?

"The Girls' Science Club, bozo," said Eddie.

"No way!" I said. "It was a total surprise. And she's not my girlfriend."

"Yeah, well it's not fair they have a science club and we don't," said Eddie. Billy nodded.

"I want to go on TV," Billy said.

This was not how the field trip was supposed to go. I had cans of pop and Cheetos. I had a whole package of Oreos and my Swiss Army knife. I had a flashlight, six Superman comic books, and to make things exciting, half a string of firecrackers that I'd bought at the Puyallup Indian Reservation last year. I also had a compact professional-quality video camera. I figured now was a good time to pull it out. "Check this out, guys."

"Whoa!" said Eddie when I unzipped the camera case. "Your mom lets you use the video camera?" He was impressed, I could tell.

"Yeah, anytime I want," I lied. It wasn't even ours. It belonged to the university. Mom would kill me if she knew I had it. Eddie snatched the camera out of my hands.

"Watch it!" I said. I grabbed for the camera,

but Eddie danced away from me and held it high.

"Just let me look, okay?" he said with a grin. "Please?"

"Okay, okay," I said. Eddie looked through the camera. "You can't see anything until it's turned on," I told him. I looked around.

"Take a movie of me," said Billy. "I want to be on TV."

"No, Wigman's going to take a movie of both of us, right?" I took the camera from Eddie and let out a huge sigh of relief.

"Yeah, but let's go a little farther," I said. I was sure I could still hear my mom's voice nearby in the woods.

"You follow us," said Eddie, "with the camera. Take a live movie, you know, while we go looking for animal things. It'll be good practice for when we go on TV for real." I checked for spies one more time. A blue jay flew past. The coast was clear. Even if they were determined to be in on the contest maybe we could still goof around. They were sure excited about that camera, which had been part of my original plan. Everything looked extra fuzzy through the viewfinder, but it wasn't hard to find the guys. I pointed my finger at them and they started to talk.

"Okay," said Eddie, "we're on this nature walk and we're looking for stuff for our collections." He held up a plastic bag. "So we can massacre the girls."

"Yeah," said Billy, walking away but turning his head so he could see me. "Wigman's mom wants us to find a bunch of pinecones. Okay. So here we go looking." He and Eddie stopped and kicked over a rock. Billy bent over with his rear end pointing right at the camera. I zoomed in on it, trying hard not to laugh. Now, that I could see. It filled the screen.

"Nothin' under this rock," said Billy, "but it's a nice view anyway." I cracked up and it jiggled the camera a little. Eddie made a face.

"Get serious, Chili," said Eddie. "I want to win this thing." They shoved each other and actually looked around, like they were looking for signs of wildlife.

"Keep going, you guys," I said. They continued down the trail, looking under bushes and eyeing the ground, until Billy started hopping and karate-kicking the tree trunks. I kept the camera rolling. Eddie found a pinecone and put it in his mouth. He crossed his eyes and blew out his cheeks. Billy poked him in the rear end with a stick and he spit the pinecone about six feet. I laughed and the camera jiggled again.

I took a deep breath and watched the Billy and Eddie shapes in the viewfinder. They were having a great time and so was I, and no one was getting in trouble. I mean, we *were* looking for animal stuff, right? I was fitting in and I had friends again, cool friends. I reached up and fingered my plastic ear stud. The glue itched. It was still stuck tight. Maybe I could talk Mom into letting me get one ear pierced. That's what I was thinking when Eddie started to yell.

"Hey! Look at this!" said Billy. I zoomed in on another pinecone he had in his hand. "There's pieces of this pinecone all over the place. I bet a squirrel ate it for dinner or something." Billy picked up the pieces.

"Put it in the bag, man," said Eddie. "Maybe we'll get an A from Science Woman. TV, here I come! 'Hi, girls and boys,'" he mimicked. "'It's time to *JUMP* into science!'" I felt my face turn red. It bugged me that he called my mom Science Woman and made fun of the way she talked, even if I did cringe every time I heard her say it on TV. Eddie grabbed Billy's bag.

"Hey!" yelled Billy. "Give it back."

Eddie ran around a tree with Billy after him. They were laughing so hard that a couple of times I thought they'd both fall in a heap. Finally Billy had his bag of pinecone pieces back. Both boys panted and mugged for the camera.

"Me Tarzan, him Jane," said Billy, pointing at Eddie.

"Shut up," said Eddie, and then he broke into the loudest Tarzan yell you have ever heard. Billy started yelling too. The trees seemed to echo with the noise.

"You guys, *shut up!*" I said, trying not to laugh. I put the camera on PAUSE. I made my face look serious. "I'm not kidding," I said. "If you guys start yelling, someone will come over here and find out I have this camera and then—" I made a slashing motion across my throat with my free hand.

"I thought you said you get to use it whenever you want," said Eddie. I was caught. I felt my face turn red. "Did you rip it off, Wigman?"

"No!" I said. "I borrowed it."

"Liar," said Eddie with a huge grin. "I ripped off a radio once, but a camera, *cool.*" Billy stared at me and blinked. His mouth dropped open in surprise.

"I didn't steal it, Billy, honest," I said to him. I swallowed hard. I felt like a total criminal. I could tell by Billy's face that he didn't believe me.

"Okay, okay," said Eddie. "Who cares where you got it? How about you be in the movies for a while, Wigman? I can be the cameraman." He reached for the camera.

"I don't think so, Eddie," I said. I glanced over at Billy and wished I'd never brought that stupid camera.

"Come on," said Eddie.

"No, let me," said Billy. They moved toward me. No way could I let them get their hands on it.

"If it were mine I'd let you," I said lamely. Just then a weird-shaped thing on the ground caught my eye. "Hey, look!" I said. Eddie and Billy turned around. "Over there. What is that?" I rubbed my eyes and squinted to focus them. Beside a stump, on the ground, was a perfect deer antler! "You guys! An antler!" I turned the camera back on. I'd convince Billy later that I didn't rip it off. "Quick," I said. "Pick up the antler and I'll get it on film." Billy picked up the antler. It had six points. Eddie grabbed it and put it on his head.

"Check this out!" said Eddie. "We are going to win the contest now, yes boys and girls, you saw it here on Channel 4," he said. Billy picked up a pinecone and acted like it was a mike.

"Do you anticipate any reaction from the Girls' Science Club over the discovery of this antler?" Billy asked Eddie.

"Total grief and defeat," said Eddie. "ONE! TWO! THREE!" yelled Eddie. Then together, he and Billy and I all yelled, "BOYS RULE!" I turned off the camera and went to look at the antler. It still had bits of skin clinging to it. Deer shed their antlers every year. I'd always wanted to find one. I shifted the camera under one arm so I could handle the antler better. That's when Eddie snatched the camera.

"Give it back," I said. I remembered my necktie.

"I'm not going to hurt your little camera, Wigman," he said. "Come on, let's make a movie with all of us. We can fake some jump shots." He put the camera in one hand and lifted it up like it was a basketball. I held my breath.

"I thought you guys wanted to win the contest," I said. My voice sounded high. I had to get that camera back. "Just give it here, Eddie, okay? I'll set it up so we can all be in it." I gave the antler to Billy. Eddie gave me the camera and picked up a pinecone. I sighed a huge one. Then I set the camera on the stump where we'd found the antler. There was this big log resting on top of the stump. There was just enough room for the camera. The stump was dry on top, where I'd set the camera, but it was sort of slimy on the sides. The log looked half rotten. I looked through the viewfinder until I could see Eddie and Billy. They had their heads together. I couldn't hear what they were talking about. I fiddled with the buttons on the camera.

If Eddie would stop trying to take the camera, we could make a good movie. We could show it to everyone later. It was a great idea, really, a documentary of us on the field trip to Mount Rainier. I could tell Mom I'd wanted to make my own science documentary but was scared to ask about the camera. She'd forgive me for sure. We were on a class field trip, we were doing what we were supposed to *and* we were having fun. The antler was really cool. It would be hard to beat. Maybe going on my mom's show wouldn't be too bad if Eddie and Billy were there. I hadn't thought about that.

"You guys ready?" I called. "Let's make it like a funny interview." They both nodded. I pushed the REC button and hurried to join them.

"So, Mr. Wigman, how do you like the great outdoors so far?" Eddie asked me with the pinecone under my nose.

"Love it," I said. "The air is so fresh." I sucked in some air and belched it out. Eddie laughed and kept talking.

"Is it true the Boys' Science Club has just made an incredible discovery?" He waved the antler in my face. I had to dodge it.

"Uh, yeah," I said. "We found this rare antler."

Boys' Science Club? Was he kidding? Billy danced around beside me and took the antler from Eddie. He tucked the big end into his left front jeans pocket. Eddie grinned.

"What do you think about that scuzzy Girls' Science Club? Who's going to beat them?"

"We are!" I yelled.

"And, by the way, how does it feel to be on the coolest three-on-three team at Horace Mann Elementary?" asked Eddie.

"Awesome," I said. "We're unstoppable." Billy and I slapped high-five. Eddie leaned over toward Billy with his fake microphone.

"This here's Chili Billy the Rebounder," said Eddie to the make-believe audience. "Tell us, Mr. Rebounder, how does it feel to be on the same team as a science dude?"

"Oh, he's okay," said Billy into the camera. "He's got a good turn-around jump shot." I felt myself swell up with pride on the inside. My new image was working. No more nerd. OK, I was still a science dude, but didn't Eddie and Billy want to go on my mom's show? If they were cool *and* wanted to go on a science show, being a science dude couldn't be that bad.

"I'm tough," I said.

"Now you get a chance to prove it," said Eddie. "For our viewers at home." He turned toward the camera. Its red recording light was steady. "A guy isn't tough unless he does all the stuff us tough guys do." He grinned at Billy and winked. Billy grinned back and waggled his eyebrows up and down. Then Eddie whipped out an unlit cigarette he'd been hiding in his back pocket.

The antler fell out of Billy's pocket. "Hey, Wigman. Got a light?" Eddie asked me.

What happened next was totally humiliating. Eddie stuck his cigarette into my mouth. I spit it out. I shook my head and yelled, "You're crazy! We're gonna get in big trouble!"

Eddie pulled two more cigarettes out of his pocket and gave one to Billy. Then he took out a blue disposable lighter and lit their cigarettes. He inhaled and blew out the smoke. "Hey, this is a field trip," he said to the camera. "Take a deep drag, Wigman." I looked at the camera saw that red light and realized that all of this was on film. If anyone, *anyone* ever saw it and saw us with cigarettes, we'd be erasing blackboards until we were senior citizens. All of a sudden, coolness didn't seem so cool. Just then Eddie turned and looked at the camera. "Hey! I want a turn to be the cameraman," he yelled. I ran toward the camera like crazy.

Eddie was right behind me. "Get it, Eddie!" shouted Billy. I had to get to the camera before he did. This stupid video thing had gone too far and all I could think of was destroying that tape and forgetting I'd ever had the stupid idea of bringing that camera along. Just a couple more feet.

I reached for it.

I grabbed it.

I felt Eddie's hands on my sweatshirt. I jerked sideways and ducked under the fallen tree to get away. Passing under the tree I bumped it hard with my back. The big tree shuddered. I felt myself falling backward, I held the camera high and twisted around as my butt and then my back hit the ground. I watched in slow motion as the rotten tree trunk crashed down onto Eddie and pinned him to the ground.

Chapter Twelve

Eddie yelled. My stomach jumped into my throat. I set the camera down and scrambled over to the fallen log.

"Are you okay?" I asked. He was breathing hard, grunting and trying to twist his body. "Are you hurt?" He stopped struggling for a second.

"No, I don't think so." His chest was heaving up and down. He was breathing fast. All the toughness had gone out of his voice. "Nothing hurts, but I'm stuck. I'm *stuck!*" His voice squeaked. I got down low so I could get a good look at him. His face was white. He fought the log. It didn't move.

Eddie had fallen into a scooped-out spot on the ground. The log was covering him and pinning him down, but not squashing him. It was a big log. I still don't know how I could have bumped it that hard. I tried to lift it. It was really stuck. When it fell, it rolled a little and got jammed under another broken tree. I tried to move it with my foot. Eddie coughed. "Get me out, man. Get me out!" His eyes were wide with fear.

"Billy, get over here!" I yelled. No answer. I tugged on the log. "Try pushing up," I said. Eddie pushed. The log didn't budge. "Billy!" I yelled again. I stood up and looked around. Billy was gone. The antler lay where it had dropped. The cigarettes lay on the ground beside it like white sticks. I wanted to run over and pick them up, shove them into my backpack so no one would ever see them. But Eddie started to cry.

"Hey, Eddie, it's okay," I said. "I'll get you out. I promise." A million things were going through my head. Where was Billy? Had he gone to get help? "Just don't panic, it's okay," I said. "Take deep breaths," I told him. I told myself the same thing. My whole body was in panic mode. Eddie tried to breathe deeply, but his breaths came out in big sobs. I tried to move the log again. Nothing.

If Mr. Bell came, he'd see the cigarettes. Mom would see the camera. I tried to dig my hand in under the log. Nothing happened. Eddie cried.

"Are you sure you aren't hurt?" I asked again. I remember how sometimes people can get some terrible injury without feeling it for a while. Eddie shook his head.

"No, I told you," he sobbed. "Nothing hurts. I'm just stuck. And I'm *freezing*!" He struggled really hard, trying to scoot out from underneath by digging in his heels.

"Be quiet and let me think," I said. I had to think. I had to figure this out, and fast. And I didn't need Eddie freaking out on me. I didn't need Mom and Mr. Bell finding me like this. Eddie quieted down. I heard voices. I froze and hoped they wouldn't see me.

"Look at that antler!" It was Callie's voice.

"Eeeew, gross," said another girl's voice. "Someone littered cigarettes." I peeked up over the stump. Elise Emmenthal was poking at the cigarettes with her foot. The other girls of the Girls' Science Club were examining the antler.

"We'll win for sure with this," said Bess. "Girls' Science Club rules!"

"Don't let them take it," whispered Eddie. I looked down at his pale face and red eyes.

"What?" I asked.

"The antler."

Now I was stuck. I had to get Eddie out. I had to rescue the antler. I had to get rid of the cigarettes. I had to get the stupid tape out of the video camera and get the camera back to my mom's lab without her finding out about my borrowing it. I stood up. "Get away! That's ours," I yelled. My voice startled the girls.

"Quit sneaking up on people," said Gillian.

"We found it," said Bess. "We're going to add it to our collection."

"No, we found it," I said.

"We who?" asked Callie. She had the antler in her hand.

"Me and the other guys." I remembered what Eddie had said. "From the Boys' Science Club."

"Boys' Science Club?" said Callie with a frown. "Since when are you in a science club?" She looked right at me, one hand on her hip.

"Copycats," said Elise with disgust.

"Finders, keepers," said Gillian. "Let's leave."

"Hey!" yelled Bess. She pointed to a spot on the ground. "Whose feet are those?" The girls ran over. They all spoke at once. A couple of them squealed. I told them Eddie wasn't hurt, just stuck. Eddie's face turned red. It was a good change from white.

"Aren't you going to get him out?" asked Callie.

"What do you think I've been trying to do?" I yelled. I looked right at Callie and took a deep breath. I made myself be calm. I tried to think. I couldn't think. My brain was totally fuzzed up. "I could sure use some help right now. Please?" Callie looked at me for what felt like a year. "I said I was sorry, Callie, for being a jerk. And I really meant it. Honest." She looked down at Eddie and nodded. "Honest," I said again.

"Okay," she said.

"Get Mr. Bell," yelled Eddie. "Get me outta here. Quit standing around and staring at me!" His voice shook. It was weird to see him so scared. I shoved on the tree again.

"All we have to do is move it enough for him to crawl out," I said. The girls tried to lift while I pushed. The tree moved, but not much.

"We need something to lift it up with," said Callie. "A big stick or something." She ran off and came back a second later with a long branch. We stuck the branch under the tree about a foot from Eddie and tried to pry it up. Nothing happened.

"Get a big rock," said Eddie, almost in a whisper, "to go under the branch." Of course! In all the excitement I'd spaced out on the obvious. A lever! That's what we needed. Callie and I looked at each other and then at Eddie.

"Good thinking, Einstein," said Callie. Bess and Elise dragged a rock over. Callie and I put it under the branch.

"Now," I said, "we've got to move the tree without hurting Eddie. Just enough for him to get out." Bess and Elise and Gillian stood on the opposite side of the tree to steady and guide it. Callie and I got ready to push on the lever we had put together, with Eddie's help.

"One, two, three!"

We pushed. Eddie pushed. The girls kept their hands on the tree trunk. The tree moved up a few inches, then the branch slipped and it thumped down. Eddie yelled.

"Ow! You're gonna kill me!"

"Okay, okay," I said, breathing hard and fast. My hands were sweating. Callie turned to me.

"Why don't you get down next to Eddie and make sure the branch doesn't slip out? I can push on it enough to move it."

"You're too little," I said.

"No, I can do it," she said. "I won't have to push that hard." I could see what she meant. It wasn't lifting the log so much as lifting it right that was the problem. I looked at Eddie's face. Big tears rolled from his eyes down into his ears.

"If we can get it up, I can jam something underneath to keep it up," I said. I looked around and found a rock about twice the size of my fist. I lay down on the ground beside Eddie. He was pale again.

Pale and terrified. "Okay, I'm ready." Callie pushed down on the lever. The two girls kept the log from rolling. As soon as it was three inches off the ground I tried to wedge the rock underneath. It didn't fit.

"Keep pushing, Callie! You're doing great!" I said. The log rose a bit. The rock still didn't fit. Eddie was starting to wiggle. "Not yet!" I said to him. "Wait a sec." Eddie stopped. Callie pushed. I jammed the rock underneath. "Yes!" I yelled. Callie let the log settle onto the rock. Eddie started to squirm out from under the log. I tried to pull my hand out, but my sweatshirt sleeve had slipped down past my wrist and a bit of the cuff was pinned under the rock. Eddie pulled himself free. I heard Mr. Bell yell his name. I gave my arm a very small jerk. My shoulder went into the log and pushed it. The log rolled off the rock and fell with a thump.

My arm snapped like a twig.

Chapter Thirteen

I never screamed so loud in my life. I never knew anything could hurt like breaking a bone. I actually felt it crack. The pain grabbed my arm and invaded my whole body. I could hear myself screaming. I couldn't stop. I couldn't move, except to scream.

I remember Mr. Bell grabbing that log around the middle and lifting it right off my arm. I remember thinking maybe his fat belly was pure muscle after all. I remember seeing Callie with the video camera under one arm. I don't remember exactly what happened next.

Later Mom told me Billy had come to get her and

Mr. Bell. They'd hurried as fast as they could and sent Billy to get the rangers. Instead of Eddie under a log, they found me. After Mr. Bell lifted off the tree, a ranger splinted my arm somehow. I didn't watch. I don't even remember if it was a woman or man ranger. I couldn't look, it hurt so bad.

Someone else must have driven us to town because Mom held me the whole time. Every time we hit a bump in the road I wanted to barf. The pain in my arm hammered and throbbed and sucked at my stomach. It took forever to get to the hospital. By the time we got there, I was actually hoping they'd give me a big shot, anything to get rid of the pain.

As we drove up to the emergency door, I remember thinking three things. First, I never got to drink my root beer. Second, they would probably cut off my Seahawks sweatshirt and Elvis T-shirt to fix my arm, and third, I was never going to live down all the screaming and crying. I'd be a wimp for life. I'd be a nerd forever.

For once, I didn't care.

That was a week ago today. My arm still hurts, but

I'm not taking the strong painkillers anymore, so I went to school today. Mom grounded me for a week for taking the camera, but she let it be the week I was home from school anyway. I promised I'd never do it again. I also promised I'd never Super Glue anything to my body again. Mom had to pour half a cup of acetone on my ear to get that stupid piece of plastic off.

I was nervous about going to school this morning, after crying and everything, but the first thing in the door Mr. Bell handed me a big pack of Magic Markers. He leaned over and spoke in a loud voice so everyone could hear. "I broke my leg when I was your age," he said. "I never bawled so hard in my life. Boy, did that hurt." I could have hugged him, but that would have been pretty juvenile. After that he let everyone sign my cast before we started class. Kids kept asking when my mom was going to visit our class again. I said I didn't know, but I was sure it would be soon. Turns out they really liked her, ugly glasses and all. They were disappointed she didn't get to do the dissection.

By the time almost everyone had taken a turn

signing my cast, I actually felt kind of famous. Eddie took up a big space when he wrote. My cast goes all the way to my shoulder, so there was room for it.

"Thanks for saving my life, Wiggie," it says in big yellow-and-green letters. "E. Grz." He punched me in the shoulder when he was done. The *other* shoulder.

"No prob," I said.

Billy signed my cast right after Eddie. Next to his name he wrote *amigos*.

"Amigos means friends, right?" I asked.

"Yeah," said Billy. He fiddled with the lid of the marker. "I knew you didn't steal that camera, Wiggie," he said.

"Thanks," I said, feeling happy and stupid at the same time. "Maybe when I get this cast off we can shoot some hoops in my yard," I said. "Like before."

"Cool," said Billy and slapped five with my good hand.

I found out later that right after my accident, Mr. Bell phoned ahead to Mrs. Jefferson back at school and told her what had happened. When the bus got there, Eddie's grandma and Billy's mom were waiting. And get this. The General had called in a police officer to talk to the two guys. The officer had a long meeting with all of them in the General's office. Eddie and Billy didn't tell me much except to say that the police officer was a woman, and she didn't smile once. Billy says he will never touch another cigarette. Mr. Bell didn't have to yell at either of them today.

At lunch Billy said they'd save my place on the three-on-three team until I got my cast off, because nobody else has as good a turn-around jump shot as me. Eddie said he was serious about starting a boys' science club and asked what I thought. I told him it was an awesome idea. Ryan Ellefson and Joey Kithara overheard and said they wanted to join if we did it. So did the twins, Rob and Richie Stivik. We decided to have a meeting on Saturday, at my house. Eddie said if we do have a club he should be president, since he thought of making the lever. I'll go along with that. Boys rule—some of the time anyway.

I'm learning to write left handed. Callie's left handed. She showed me how to slant my hand above the paper so I don't smear the ink. I knocked the pencil box off my desk with my elbow the first time I tried and we both laughed. Then we both bent over at the same time to pick it up and our heads clunked together really hard.

"Sorry," she said, rubbing her head and messing up one of her braids so it stuck straight out.

"No, *I'm sorry*," I said. "Honest. About everything." Callie grinned. "And thanks for helping me rescue Eddie. I couldn't have done it without your help."

"Any time," said Callie with a twinkle in her eye. "As long as you promise not to sneeze on me."

"I've given up glitter for good," I said, and then we both laughed.

As it turned out, Callie and the other girls from the Girls' Science Club ended up winning the contest, even without the antler. They'd found the upper part of a beaver's skull, complete with long orange buckteeth. It's on Mr. Bell's desk right now. Callie and Bess said they wanted to name the skull Betty, but Gillian and Elise wanted to name it Bucky. At lunch recess they were still arguing about it.

Callie signed my cast after school, right next to

where Wolfie wrote $E = mc^2$. While she was writing, I told her I was going to cheer super loud when she and the other girls go on TV with my mom next month. I told her next time, the Boys' Science Club is going to annihilate them.

"No way," she said in a mad voice, but her eyes were smiling.

I'm learning to eat left handed too. What a pain. But the good news is Mom's cooking has been improving in the last few days. She made grilled cheese for dinner two nights this week and macaroni and cheese (the box kind) last night. That's why I was so surprised to smell a strange aroma coming out of the kitchen just before dinner. Here I thought she'd turned over a new leaf. Maybe she just felt sorry for me. It was a very strong coconut and onion smell. Thailand, according to Wolfie.

I was trying to button my Levi's left handed so I could go down to eat weird-smelling food, when the doorbell rang. Foofie started barking. My stomach growled. Maybe food from Thailand wouldn't be all that bad. I heard the front door open and then I heard Mom's voice.

"Well, hello there," she said in her ultra-best friendly voice. Hmm. Definitely not the newspaper girl, Eileen. I opened my bedroom door. I sneaked to the end of the hall and spied on Mom down the stairs. "What a nice surprise, Mr. Bell." she said. "How are you tonight?"

Mr. Bell? What was *he* doing here? I held my breath and watched and listened.

"I'm just super," said Mr. Bell. He was grinning at my mom. "I was in the neighborhood and, I, uh, just wanted to tell you how nice it is to have Wiggie back at school."

"That was really nice of you," said Mom. "He was very glad to be back in class today." This was turning out to be a very nice and dumb conversation. Mr. Bell polished his bald head with one hand and sniffed the air.

"Smells like Thai food," he said.

"How did you know?" Mom said in a surprised and pleased voice.

"The delicious smell is a dead giveaway," said Mr. Bell. "Well, I'd better be going now.

He actually likes *that smell?* I thought. Bizarre.

"Why don't you stay for supper?" asked Mom. "There's plenty, and—"

No way.

"—really generous of you but I couldn't impose like that," said Mr. Bell.

"It wouldn't be an imposition at all," said Mom.

Mr. Bell? In our house? Eating my mom's weird food? I pinched myself. I was definitely awake.

"Please, Mr. Bell. We'd love to have you."

Mr. Bell took off his coat and hung it on the hook right next to Wolfie's jacket. He stuffed his hands into his pockets and puffed out his cheeks. Foofie sniffed his feet. "Please," said Mr. Bell, "call me Alex."

"All right, Alex." said Mom.

"It's short for Alexander," said Mr. Bell. "Alexander Graham Bell."

This can't be happening.

Mom started to laugh. Mr. Bell laughed too. Foofie barked.

A soft groan escaped my lips. I slumped against the wall and slid all the way down to the floor.

"Wiggie!" Mom called. "Guess who's coming to dinner?"

"I heard," I said weakly. "Hi, Mr. Bell."

I had a sneaking suspicion that my life was just about to get complicated again.